THE TRAVELING TEA LADIES

Till Death Do Us Part

Other Titles in The Traveling Tea Ladies Series

The Traveling Tea Ladies
Death in Dallas

The Traveling Tea Ladies
Death in Dixie

The Traveling Tea Ladies
Death in the Low Country

The Traveling Tea Ladies
Till Death Do Us Part

Other Books by Melanie O'Hara

Savannah Skies
Return to Tybee Island

Here's what readers are saying about The Traveling Tea Ladies

"As owner of The Tea Academy and Miss Melanie's Tea Room & Gourmet Tea Emporium, Melanie O'Hara has made a seamless foray into murder and mayhem set among tea enthusiasts in the South. Her primary women characters, Amelia, Olivia, Cassandra and Sarah, combine sophistication with compassion and eccentricity as they drink tea in Amelia's Victorian tea room, experiment with delectable recipes and juggle jobs, family, social calendars and shopping. Their trip from the sleepy town of Dogwood Cove, Tennessee, to the big city of Dallas for a girl's weekend exceeds their expectations for "adventure" when murder is unexpectedly added to the menu. In the tradition of the British cozy mystery, *The Traveling Tea Ladies* blends quirky characters, good food and drink with mystery and intrigue."

Judy Slagle, Department Chair of Literature and Languages
East Tennessee State University

"Talk about a perfect book to read at the beach ... entertaining and intriguing! Melanie O'Hara is a young woman whose background of owning a tea room has provided the perfect experiences for her unique books about *The Traveling Tea Ladies!*

The Traveling Tea Ladies Death in Dixie is a story that shows the deep friendships and loyalty of four friends who share an acute interest in tea. I found myself making notes of certain types of tea to try and could almost taste some of the tea foods and candy the author described.

This second book of Melanie's does make you wonder what can happen to these creative and resourceful women's next. I can't wait—the next book will take place in Savannah!"

Kathy Knight
ACCENT Editor, *The Greeneville Sun*

"Melanie O'Hara opens the door on unexpected intrigue from the genteel tea rooms of East Tennessee. The mystery is steeped in local color as the tea ladies muster their forces to help a friend in need. Readers will want to put a pot on and do some traveling themselves."

Randall Brown
Writer, Knoxville News Sentinel

"I guarantee that once you start this book you will not be able to put it down. In fact I was so connected to the storyline that I almost missed my train stop. Rarely do I find a book that can capture my attention so deeply that I forget I am riding to work on the noisy NYC subway. I highly recommend this book. It's perfect for a book club or to give your best friend as a gift. Every time I sat down to read this book I felt I was getting together with my closest friends. It is a true gem indeed. I cannot wait to read about the next adventure the Traveling Tea Ladies take on."

Patty Aizaga
NYCGirlAtHeart.com

THE TRAVELING TEA LADIES

Till Death Do Us Part

Melanie O'Hara

LYONS
LEGACY
PUBLISHING™

Johnson City, Tennessee

The Traveling Tea Ladies™
'Till Death Do Us Part

Cover art by Susi Galloway
www.SusiGalloway.com

Book design by Longfeather Book Design
www.longfeatherbookdesign.com

You may contact the publisher at:
Lyons Legacy Publishing™
123 East Unaka Aveneue
Johnson City, Tennessee 37601
Publisher@LyonsLegacyPublishing.com

ISBN: 978-0-9836145-3-1

For Charlie
You came into the world
Bringing peace and light to my life
You continue to be a source
Of pride and joy
I love you very much.

ACKNOWLEDGEMENTS

This book was a joy for me to write from start to finish because I LOVE weddings! But even projects filled with excitement take work and I have many people I would like to recognize.

I humbly express my gratitude to Phyllis Estepp for her expertise in editing. Once again, she has saved me from blunders and mishaps! Your enthusiasm for the characters and the storyline keep spurring me to write.

Love and kisses to my "Real-Life Shane Spencer," my husband Keith who made our wedding the most romantic day of my life. For your countless hours of patience in tolerating wedding shows, reading over my manuscripts, and offering outstanding ideas, I thank you and love you always.

I am blessed to have wonderful children who are so generous; they haven't voiced opposition to having characters based on them. I am still amazed that God blessed me with you.

A special thank you to Erik and Robert Jacobson for excellence in book design. I appreciate your precision and expertise.

Much appreciation to Susi Galloway for bringing the ladies to life with your charming artwork.

And finally, THANK YOU to all who have taken this tea journey with me. I have so enjoyed getting to know the readers of the series and pinch myself every day that I am supported by such devoted friends. I look forward to many more tea adventures with all of you.

THE TRAVELING TEA LADIES

Till Death Do Us Part

ONE

*I*t was a gorgeous fall day in our Tennessee mountain town of Dogwood Cove, the kind of blissfully perfect day where the skies were sapphire blue and the sun was intense. The Southern Appalachian Mountains wrapped around our town as far as the eye could see. A few wispy clouds sat like cotton candy atop the majestic wonders and I was very grateful to live in an area surrounded by so much beauty.

I had enjoyed what might possibly be the last warm day I could drive with my rag top down on "lady bug." I expertly pulled up to the curb in front of Gail's Bridal Boutique and parallel parked my lipstick red VW beetle. I glanced in the rearview mirror to smooth my shoulder length dark blonde hair, which appeared rather disheveled and windblown after the short drive from our house to Main Street.

I was in a rush to meet Cassandra for Olivia's final fitting of her wedding gown. It had been quite an ordeal getting Olivia to even consider a wedding instead of eloping, let alone select a dress. But our resident "fashionista" Cassandra had prevailed and Olivia was in the midst of final preparations for her nuptials to Detective Matt Lincoln, AKA "Lincoln."

I dashed into the bridal salon just in time to hear the objections coming from our frazzled cowgirl sequestered in the rear of the shop.

"I feel like Scarlett O'Hara being cinched up for the BBQ at Five Oaks!" Olivia complained as the wedding shop attendant carefully laced the corseted gown in the secluded dressing room. "I certainly wouldn't have picked this one if I had known it was going to take so long to get in and out of it! How am I supposed to mount Maggie May feeling like I've been bound like King Tut?" the exasperated five foot tall red head spewed from the back room.

"Quit your whining and get out here so we can all see you!" Cassandra snapped at her best friend. "Gosh you are making all of us a nervous wreck today! Hello, Amelia. Thank goodness Gail has been nice enough to serve us all champagne. That's the only way I can survive the ordeal of this wedding dress fitting," she confided as she took a sip.

"Cassandra, don't make things worse on her," I beseeched my close friend as I greeted her with a hug. She was dressed from head to toe in a bright canary yellow Armani pant suit. To complete the designer look, she was carrying a black patent Chanel clutch with matching stilettos.

"Olivia's going to need our support, especially today. You know how tense she has been about her family arriving tonight. We've got to find a way to help her relax. Maybe our bride needs a glass of champagne too?" I suggested.

"I second that, Amelia!" Olivia said as she came out of the dressing room. I felt my breath catch in my throat as I admired the beautiful bride standing before me. Though she had both hands on her hips and looked perturbed, Olivia

Rivers did make one stunning bride. The dress flattered her body type perfectly. The candlelight white satin gown had a sweet heart neckline. The mermaid cut was cinched in at her midline and flared out around her calves. It emphasized her curves in all the right places. It was the perfect dress for her and I knew her fiancé would love it.

"Drink up, *Bridezilla*. Have a glass of champagne so we can all enjoy today," Cassandra joked as she handed Olivia a flute of bubbly. Her chin length platinum hair moved with each exaggerated gesture as she spoke.

"I am not *a Bridezilla!*" Olivia said defensively. "I'm simply trying to survive the multiple check lists Dixie insists upon. I should have thought twice about using *your wedding planner*," she fussed as she took a sip of champagne.

"Dixie Beauregard is one of *the best*," Cassandra reminded her. "I had to pull some major strings to get her to move your wedding up six months to October! You don't appreciate how much she is in demand. You do realize she did Nick Cannon and Mariah Carey's wedding? They are still talking about the reception in *People Magazine*.

"I don't care whose wedding she's done! She's driving me nuts! Her 'uber' organization is on my last nerve. I feel like every minute of my day has been carefully orchestrated and triple checked. I feel like I have to ask permission to take a bathroom break," she concluded as she took another sip of her champagne.

"You look lovely, Liv!" I said as I wiped tears from my eyes. "I'm so glad you chose that gown. It's perfect!"

"Thanks, Amelia," Olivia said as she stepped up on the pedestal and stood before the three way mirror. "You don't think it's too much?" she asked as she ran her hands down the front of the dress. She carefully adjusted the veil and continued scrutinizing her attire.

"No, not at all," I replied reassuringly. "Lincoln will love this dress on you."

"I don't know. I just don't feel comfortable in it. I want to make sure it says 'me,'" she continued as she surveyed herself in the mirror. Worry was etched all over her face.

"You're used to Wranglers and plaid shirts. Your wedding day is the one day you should look every part the bride," Cassandra said knowingly.

And she should know. Cassandra had been on Dogwood Cove's 'Top Ten Best Dressed List' the past eleven years. With her high-powered connections, it was not unusual to see her at Fashion Week in New York, shopping in Paris or Milan. Cassandra Reynolds was, after all, the CEO of Reynolds' Candies, and she made sure she dressed the part. Fashion was just one of her many talents.

"How am I supposed to ride in on Maggie May wearing this tight laced up corset? I didn't think this one through," Olivia thought aloud.

The wedding was being held in just a few days at Riverbend Ranch. Olivia was planning on riding her favorite mare, Maggie May, to the ceremony, which was being held outdoors. She had to halt this week's riding lessons while the ranch was being transformed for the big day by Cassandra's event planner Dixie Beauregard and her large staff. Olivia referred to Dixie's creative team as the "pixies" because she felt they had invaded every aspect of her home and life much like a termite infestation, in her opinion.

"You can ask Dan and the ranch hands to help you get on and off Maggie May," I suggested as I straightened and fluffed the train on her dress. I couldn't help but choke back the tears as I admired the beautiful bride. It was a wonder with her head strong ways that Olivia had found someone who was also tough enough to enter a partnership and stand toe-to-toe with her. Matt Lincoln had softened and brought out the best in my dear friend. This union was a good thing for both of them.

"Oh, I'm sure Dan and the others would get a kick out of that! I've never had to ask them to do anything I couldn't do myself," the independent ranch owner joked as she looked over her shoulder in the mirror.

"A wedding dress does put you at a disadvantage. I'd take the help, though," Cassandra reasoned. "You know the guys love Lincoln and they are working hard to clear out the barn and get the grounds ready. They'll do anything for you, Liv."

Cassandra was right about that. Dan and the ranch hands at Riverbend Ranch respected Olivia, not just because she was the owner, but because she worked side-by-side with them. She baled hay, bush hogged fields, roped calves, shoed horses and did the dozens of chores required for running a ranch. This little lady could work circles around most men *and* eat them under the table, yet somehow she managed to maintain her petite frame.

She was also respected in the community for her work with 'handi-capable' children in Dogwood Cove. Olivia ran a therapeutic horseback riding center in which she matched horses with children's needs. The bond between horse and rider was magical to witness and the program had been quite successful. She was a wonderful asset to our small Northeast Tennessee community.

"I wouldn't change a thing, Liv!" I gushed over her dress. "What do you think, Gail?"

"I think it's stunning. I'll have it ready to be picked up Friday morning, all pressed and bagged for you," the bridal shop owner beamed. "You are going to be a beautiful bride!"

"Thank you, Gail. You have been so easy to work with," Olivia hugged her. "I wish I could say that about everyone," she stated with a mischievous look in her eye.

The bells on the wedding shop door jingled as a brisk breeze blew fallen leaves into the store entryway.

"Speak of the devil," Olivia grimaced. "Here she is wearing Prada!"

"Oh, Doll Baby! Let me take a look at you!" Dixie Beauregard called out as she approached our group. She was dressed in a Burberry plaid cape over skintight black leggings and thigh high ebony riding boots. A cloud of Marc Jacob cologne enveloped the entire shop as she embraced Cassandra in a warm hug. She was carrying her white Shih Tzu, Trixie, in a matching Burberry dog carrier. The little dog poked its head around and gauged her surroundings. Dixie whipped off her oversized Gucci sunglasses to scrutinize the dress.

"O-LI-V-IA! You look magnificent!" she squealed as she grasped Olivia's hands and spun her around. "Wait until that man of yours sees you in this! You will bring tears to his eyes! So we're good here, then, Gail? I can check off the dress?" She did not wait for the bridal ship owner's response before continuing. "I'm here to remind the bride you need to leave in approximately ten minutes if you are going to make it to your bridal tea on time," she said checking her day planner.

"The bride cannot be late for her own shower, now can she? Chop, chop!"

"See what I mean, Gail?" Olivia commented as she stepped down from the pedestal. "You think you can get me out of this dress in ten minutes?" she asked as she headed back to the dressing room.

"We'll do our best," Gail calmly responded and smiled following her down the hallway.

I was tickled at the scene before me. Dixie seemed oblivious to the fact that she annoyed Olivia to no end. If she did know, I supposed it mattered not much to her. She was driven in every aspect of her business from her long check lists, to her radio ear buds she insisted all of her team members wear. She was on top of everything and I had to admire her dedication, even if it bordered on obsessive at times. But, that is exactly why she was so sought after by the big-name celebrities and politicians.

"Now, Cassandra, you, Amelia and Sarah have had your final fittings for your bridesmaids' gowns," Dixie stated more than asked. "I just want to remind you that we will all meet Saturday morning at ten o'clock for hair and makeup at Armando's. Wear something that unbuttons in the front so you don't undo his magic when you change clothes. We'll have your dresses waiting at the farmhouse so you can all get ready following your appointment. Any questions?" she asked efficiently.

"No. None that I can think of," I responded and looked at Cassandra.

"I've got everything under control for the rehearsal dinner Friday night," Cassandra volunteered. "Chef Anne Burrell is flying in to prepare the meal. She's my surprise for

Olivia. It's going to be quite an evening!" Cassandra whispered excitedly.

"That reminds me, the rehearsal is at five o'clock sharp. I expect you to be there early if at all possible," Dixie chastised us. "Well, let's get the bride rolling and let's get on to the bridal tea!" she shouted snapping her day planner closed.

"I'm coming, I'm coming! Thanks Gail," Olivia cried over her shoulder. "I'll see you Friday to pick up the dress."

"Bye ladies!" Gail called out as we exited the bridal shop and walked over to Cassandra's Mercedes parked along Main Street.

"Ride with us, Amelia. There's no sense in taking two cars. I'll bring you back after the shower," Cassandra rationalized. She quickly pushed the remote to open the doors as we piled inside for the short drive to the Pink Dogwood Tea Room.

The tea room was owned and operated by our good friend, Sarah McCaffrey, who also happened to be one of Olivia's bridesmaids and the fourth member of our group, "The Traveling Tea Ladies." We inherited the nickname because everywhere our tea travels took us, mayhem seemed to ensue.

"Dixie irritates me to no end with her blasted schedule! And what's up with bringing Trixie everywhere? I just don't get it! I feel sorry for the poor dog. She should be out running with the border collies at my ranch. Keeping a little dog in a handbag! It's ridiculous," Olivia vented.

"Olivia, Trixie is not unhappy. She loves being taken everywhere. That dog is treated better than most people," Cassandra said defending her event planner.

"That's my point; she's a dog, not a fashion accessory. Dogs are meant to run and play, not wear designer outfits," she maintained. "Who started this fashion trend anyway? Wasn't it Paris Hilton?"

"In Hollywood and New York, dogs are extensions of their owners. It's very fashionable. I for one think Trixie is adorable."

"Of course you would, 'Victoria Beckham'!" Olivia joked. "I guess I'm not fashionable and I'm fine with that!"

Don't let the bickering between these two fool you. They are the very best of friends. In fact, Cassandra was asked to be Olivia's matron-of-honor. If it were not for her, Olivia might not have given Matt Lincoln a second thought. Cassandra recognized a well-made match and was instrumental in helping the couple realize they were meant to be together.

It was Cassandra's love life that could use an intervention right now. Her husband, Doug, was serving as a Representative in the Tennessee House of Congress. Rumor had it he might be running for Senate after his first term. He was infrequently home at their lake house and spent a good portion of his time in Nashville. Though the two had been a couple since their early days as co-eds at the University of Tennessee, it seemed they were drifting further and further apart. There had been talk about his campaign manager, Penelope Phillips, and many late nights "strategizing." Their problems had definitely taken a toll on Cassandra who had confided to me that she was going to counseling in the hopes of saving her marriage.

"Would it not be more beneficial if Doug attended the counseling with you?" I had privately asked her at a lunch just last week. "I don't see how you can work on your marriage if only half of the couple is there."

"Amelia, Doug thinks counseling is a waste of time. It helps me to have someone to talk with and give me insight. I've exhausted myself trying to figure out what is wrong. I can only fix me and I'm only in control of me," she quietly cried and dabbed her eyes. "I'm doing all I can to save my marriage. But enough of that, let's talk about Olivia's wedding shower," she quickly composed herself and was all business after her brief break down.

I knew better than to overstep my bounds with Cassandra. She was a very private person and the little bit she had confided to me was more than what was comfortable for her. If she was talking about her marriage, there was definitely trouble.

Cassandra Reynolds was the real power behind Reynolds' Candies, a third generation company started by Doug's grandfather. If Doug didn't realize how invaluable she was, he was not a competent business person. I was beginning to have a negative opinion of him and his recent behavior.

"She's not bringing that dog into the 'Pink Lady?'" Olivia asked flabbergasted as she watched Dixie exit her Land Rover with Trixie in her dog carrier. "Surely Sarah will not permit animals in her restaurant!"

"Sarah is allowing Trixie to stay in the fenced side garden where she will be safe. It's all been arranged," I reassured her. "She'll have a ball playing with Lily." Lily was the tiger striped tabby and official mascot of the Pink Dogwood Tea Room. She even had her own blog and fan club. In my opinion, every tea room needed a porch kitty. She would hold her own with Trixie.

"There you are!" Sarah greeted us as we pulled in front of the historic Victorian tea room and parked along the street. "You look beautiful, Liv! Come on in," she hugged and greeted each of us effusively.

Sarah had outdone herself today though I was really not surprised. She had been doing an outstanding job of running the tea room ever since she purchased the one hundred eight year old home from us last year. It had been a hard decision for my husband Shane Spencer and me to sell the tea room, but our online tea and coffee wholesale business had taken off much faster than we had anticipated. Running two businesses had become too much for us to handle as well as raising a family.

We were relieved that Sarah had approached us when we put the pink Victorian up for sale. She loved the tea room as much as we did. Any time you own a business, it is an extension of yourself. Sarah would take good care of our "baby." We were now able to devote our attention to Smoky Mountain Coffee, Herb and Tea Company and spend more time with our children, Charlie and Emma, confident that we had made the right decision.

Prior to owning the tea room, Sarah had served as the children's librarian for Dogwood Cove's public library. She had made a seamless foray into the tea world and incorporated some of her favorite literary classics into themed tea parties, such as *Anne of Green Gables, Pride and Prejudice and Little Women*. Sarah had infused so much of her creativity and spirit into the business and I was very proud of her.

"Goodness, Sarah! This place looks amazing," I cried as I entered the hallway. The curved staircase banister was covered in a garland of Olivia's favorite sunflowers scattered with clusters of red pepper berries and loose bows of raffia. The sideboard in the entry way was decorated with a montage of framed pictures of the happy couple. It was a clever idea and also served as a housewarming gift from Sarah for the bride and groom.

The bold color scheme of gold and burgundy was carried into the dining room where tables of six were set with saffron damask tablecloths crowned with ruby red chargers. The centerpieces were trios of glass cylinders filled with cranberries and pomegranates. Each was topped with gilded floating candles. The effect was stunning. From the Waterford crystal water goblets to the gold plated silverware, Sarah had seen to every detail.

"Sarah, this is stunning!" Olivia gasped as she looked around the room. "How did you know exactly what I wanted? I didn't even imagine something this nice. Thank you!" Olivia excitedly hugged her dear friend.

"It has been my pleasure, Liv! I just visualized what I wanted for my bridal shower and thought about your colors and it just all came together. I'm glad you like it!" Sarah beamed under the praise. "I wasn't sure if you would think the gold was a 'bit much,' but I think it suits you!"

"It does suit her," Cassandra agreed. She ran her fingers through her chin length hair and placed her hand on her hip. "I've been trying to get Olivia to buy this gorgeous gold satin evening gown for her honeymoon, but she thinks it's too upscale for her 'prairie girl' collection," she playfully joked.

Cassandra had helped ease Olivia into her 'inner diva,' getting Olivia to branch out from her comfortable ranch clothes into some more colorful Santa Fe inspired skirts and jewelry. Cassandra had even managed to talk her into a few purchases at Fashion Week in New York. Olivia was gradually incorporating some of her new pieces into her wardrobe and the change was not lost on Matt Lincoln. Despite Cassandra's best efforts, she couldn't get Olivia to part with her favorite red ostrich boots. Olivia wore them with everything!

"Who are you calling 'prairie girl?' I'll have you know that I have purchased some beautiful gold slingbacks for the honeymoon, just in case I decide to buy that dress," she informed us.

"You're a knockout with your auburn spiral curls in that gold halter dress," Dixie agreed as she entered the dining room, Trixie not in tow this time. "I agree one hundred percent with Cassandra. You need to buy that dress!"

"Thanks for the input, Dixie," Olivia said sounding slightly annoyed. "Does she eavesdrop on every conversation?" she turned and quietly whispered to us.

"I like Dixie," I told Olivia. "She's doing a good job of paying close attention to her client and constantly reassuring her that she *is* a knockout. I already know you are, I'm just not paid to say it," I teased my friend, hoping she would lighten up a bit and really enjoy her shower.

"Good one, Amelia!" Olivia retorted.

"Right this way, ladies and our guest of honor," Sarah cooed as she escorted us to our tables.

"Hey, Sarah, why don't I lend you a hand in the kitchen?" I offered. "It will be like old times for me!"

"Are you sure, Amelia? I would enjoy your company, but today you are a guest at the shower," she said thoughtfully. I knew Sarah wouldn't mind if I helped. Besides, there were some things I missed about being in the tea room kitchen.

"I've got plenty of time to visit with everyone," I pointed out. "You and I might have some fun. Hand me an apron. Some habits are hard to break!"

We left Cassandra, Olivia and Dixie to greet the guests and walked into the kitchen located in the back of the house. The twelve foot ceilings and soaring windows always took me back in time and made me feel at home. The tin ceiling, the marble counter tops and the built-in cabinetry always reminded me that they don't make homes with this attention to detail anymore.

"Gosh, I've missed being here," I admitted to Sarah. Just the aromas of the teas steeping and the scones baking in the oven made my blood pressure drop. It was my favorite form of aromatherapy.

"I'm sure the 'Pink Lady' has missed you too. It's good to have capable hands in the kitchen with me today," she said graciously. She looked sweet wearing the signature burgundy and cream toile tea room aprons, carrying on a tradition I had started when I opened the tea room doors more than seven years ago.

"What would you like me to do? Should I get the tea pots ready?" I thought aloud as I glanced around the kitchen.

"You can go ahead and line them up, but I think we should wait until the majority of the guests arrive to begin steeping it so the tea will be nice and hot," Sarah said decisively.

I opened up the towering cabinet doors and began carefully removing the Royal Albert tea pots. There was an assortment of country rose and the busy chintz patterns that I was so fond of. It coordinated beautifully with the green cameo plates and tea cups in jewel tones.

I lined the teapots on the counter of the 'tea bar' that we had specially designed many years ago for the tea preparation area. The counter was wide enough to hold the industrial hot pots that boiled the water and then held it at a constant temperature for proper tea preparation. Often times the difference between a good pot of tea and an amazing pot of tea is the right water temperature for each variety of tea.

The "tea bar" was lined with airtight canisters that held each tea selection. The Pink Dogwood Tea Room had a reputation for carrying over sixty varieties at any given time, not including the seasonal teas that Sarah ordered from us for Christmas and Valentine's Day. It was truly a tea lover's paradise!

When I owned the Pink Dogwood Tea Room, I insisted each server was intimately familiar not only with proper tea preparation, but in tea tasting as well. They were fully prepared to give recommendations to our guests and were willing to share their personal favorites. Sarah had carried on that crucial training and often invited me to conduct tastings if she had a team member to train or a new tea to introduce to everyone. It was one of my favorite duties as owner of Smoky Mountain Coffee, Herb and Tea Company. I was constantly surrounded by wonderful smelling teas and had the most pleasant task of tasting every one for its own unique subtle nuances.

"What are you serving today, Sarah?" I asked getting the recycled paper filters ready to fill with the gourmet loose tea.

"I'm featuring two teas today. With the first, I wanted to introduce something I think Olivia will enjoy this time of year, something to remind her of fall and her wedding, so I chose the apple Ceylon for its autumnal notes. The second tea has a more romantic flavor and will complement the beautiful red tones of the table settings."

"Let me guess—Indian summer fruit tea!" I shouted.

"How did you know?" Sarah asked amazed.

"Great minds think alike. Everyone will love that one in particular."

"And it makes the most beautiful deep pink tea. It just makes me happy!" Sarah sighed and adjusted her red Sally Jesse Raphael style glasses.

"Everything OK with you, Sarah? That was a deep sigh," I asked reading more into that sigh than Sarah had intended to reveal.

"I guess all the wedding preparations have me wondering if I will ever get married. I want to more than anything, but I just can't seem to find the right guy," Sarah admitted. She smiled weakly at me.

"You will when you're not looking. That's what I've always been told. It was true for me when I met Shane. The last thing I wanted was a boyfriend or a fiancé when we met," I reminded her.

"Yeah, Jett Rollins really messed with your head," Sarah remembered. And he did. Finding Jett in bed with my college roommate, Katherine Gold had really devastated me. But that seemed like a lifetime ago. Shane and I were happily married and had two beautiful children. I couldn't imagine my life without them. Sarah deserved that too.

"I thought you were dating that nice guy you met at church. Wasn't he going to be your date for the wedding?"

"I don't know about Richard. He's alright. There is no spark between us and I don't want to give him the wrong idea by inviting him to the wedding. It could put ideas in his head that I have romantic feelings towards him," Sarah admitted.

"I know what you mean. You don't want to send the wrong signals and then have him stuck to you like glue. It might be good for you to go to the wedding solo. You never know who you might meet. Matt may have some good-looking single friends attending," I laughed and teased her.

"Wouldn't that be something if he had a handsome brother? Then Olivia and I could be sisters-in-law," Sarah giggled.

I worried about my sweet single friend. Last year she had broken up with Jake White after a long courtship. We all thought they would get married, but Sarah realized he was a "mama's boy" and that a marriage to Jake was a marriage to 'mama.' We were all a bit relieved when she ended the relationship. She had not had good luck in the love department lately. I knew someone would discover her wonderful qualities and truly appreciate her.

"Sarah, there are about ten guests here now," Gretchen announced as she peeked her head through the kitchen door. "Hi Amelia! Your Aunt Imogene and Lucy Lyle are here too."

"Hi Gretchen, I'm so glad to see you," I said as I gave my favorite server a hug. "How have you been?"

"I'm doing great, Amelia. It's good to see you back in the kitchen. I better help seat everyone. I'll be back for the teas," she added as she exited the kitchen.

"She's so wonderful," I told Sarah. "I'm glad everyone stayed on after you took over."

"Gretchen has been wonderful. It was a good idea to promote her to manager since we've had to hire a few new people to keep up with the bigger lunch crowds," Sarah said shaking her head. "I didn't realize that running the tea room was such a fulltime job! I'm happy to be busy, believe me, but it can take over your life. Promoting Gretchen has given me some much needed rest!"

"Yes, I agree. That was a wise decision. I think people assume that when you own a tea room, the owner sits with the guests and enjoys afternoon tea every day. I always had to remind myself to take a tea break and now and then. It's great that you have decided to give yourself time off," I acknowledged. I filled the tea pots with hot water to preheat them as we talked.

"It's hard because I live upstairs. I find it's best if I leave the house for the day. Otherwise, I find reasons to come downstairs and work. I've had to establish boundaries for my personal life and work life. That hasn't been easy for me," she confessed.

"Have you had anyone knocking at your door after hours?" I inquired as I began measuring the loose tea and placing it into the filters. I filled the tea pots and replaced the lids while I set the timers to four minutes to properly steep the two featured teas.

"That happened Christmas Day, as a matter of fact," Sarah informed me. "There was a lady who wanted to see the inside of the tea room even though it was a holiday. I had to politely inform her we were closed. That didn't go over well," Sarah said as she began adding fresh flowers to garnish the tea tray.

"Stick to your guns and your boundaries. You've learned the ropes fast! Your tea trays look amazing. What's on the menu today?"

"The heart shaped savories are sweetheart sandwiches. They are filled with a wonderful herb cream cheese spread topped with thinly sliced cucumbers," Sarah said with delight in her voice.

"They are gorgeous! You are so creative," I said in awe. "And the individual yellow and red pepper quiches complement the table color scheme perfectly."

"Thanks for noticing! I'm also serving mini smoked turkey and cranberry panini's with a tea cup filled with butternut squash soup. I'm dolloping crème fraiche and sprinkling a bit of nutmeg to add a fall flavor," she announced rather proudly.

"Sarah, it's perfect. Olivia will appreciate your efforts and I for one will enjoy eating them! You thought of everything," I told her as I rushed over to turn off the timers and pull the tea filters out of the pots. The wafting smells of cinnamon and apple delighted my senses and I smiled at the thought of enjoying this beautiful tea.

"I haven't even shown you my scones yet! Wait until you sink your teeth into these beauties-cranberry orange with orange honey butter. Pure bliss!" she bragged. "The organic white clover honey is from Olivia's bee hives at Riverbend Ranch."

"I love the flavor combination. They are beautiful!" I told Sarah as she pulled them out of the double ovens. The scones had puffed up and split in the middle. "I think this bridal tea is going to be just the thing to ease Olivia's tensions.

Little did I know that Olivia's blood pressure was about to rise sky high. It's ironic how family members can either be your biggest support system or your biggest obstacle. We were about to become acquainted with the Rivers' family dynamics!

TWO

*E*mily and Gretchen did an excellent job of circulating around the tea room and keeping all the tea cups filled, which was no small feat with thirty-five guests. The Indian summer fruit tea was a favorite among everyone, but the new apple Ceylon oolong was a strong contender. It paired perfectly with the cranberry-orange scones and was a good choice.

Olivia was enjoying all the attention and seemed to be relaxing a little as long as Dixie stayed on the other side of the dining room. Sarah had thought of everything right down to the place cards on the tables. She had seated the overbearing event planner at the end of the room, farthest away from the bride. So far her strategy was working and Olivia was enjoying the bridal party games and festive atmosphere.

"Is that hunk of a man dropping by this afternoon, I'm hoping? Imogene asked Olivia. "I am in need of my daily dose of eye candy today!"

"Aunt Imogene! What has gotten into you?" I scolded shaking my head as I refilled her tea cup.

"Well, it's no secret that Olivia is marrying one of the best looking men in Dogwood Cove," Imogene playfully replied.

She was dressed from head to toe today in a leopard wrap dress with a plunging neckline. She was wearing her latest trendy purchase, leopard inspired suede boots with four inch heels. Between her ample bosoms was a large pendant in the shape of a jaguar with amber eyes. She was no shrinking violet and one of the most active seventy-year -olds I knew. She was addicted to Twitter and Facebook and had more than four hundred followers to prove it. It was no wonder she was a million dollar realtor. She was a renowned gossip and often nosy, but I loved her youthful spirit and was proud to call her family.

"Thank you Imogene. I would have to agree with you. I'm one lucky girl," Olivia said patting her hands. These two were close and kindred spirits when it came to speaking their minds. I think that's why they got along so well.

"I'll tell you what has gotten into her. She's discovered *Telemundo*," Lucy Lyle spoke up. She and Imogene had recently sold their homes in nearby historic Jonesborough and had purchased a home together in Dogwood Cove's newest subdivision, Crystal Springs. Lucy had recently turned her well established tea business, Lyla's Tea Room, over to her niece Darla so she could spend more time traveling and enjoying life. She had been a big supporter of Smoky Mountain Coffee, Herb and Tea and had been one of our best customers.

"*Telemundo*? As in the Spanish soap opera?" Olivia asked surprised.

"Yes *Telemundo*. I find it quite riveting," Imogene stated while dropping a sugar cube into her cup and stirring her tea.

"Oh, Imogene! What fun! I didn't know you spoke Spanish," Sarah smiled as she placed a tea cup full of butternut squash soup in front of each guest.

"She doesn't speak a word of Spanish. That's what makes it so funny!" Lucy remarked. "She just likes looking at those actors who remind her of Antonio Banderas."

"You don't have to understand the language to understand what's going on. I can follow it just fine," she assured us as she shot Lucy a look that could kill.

I got tickled just listening to the two of them bicker. Shane and I said it reminded us of Cassandra and Olivia and what they would be like in their golden years.

"Maybe you should order 'Rosetta Stone' so you can learn the language," Olivia continued the ribbing.

"Maybe you should hush and eat your soup before it gets cold," Imogene laughed and playfully smacked her much younger friend.

"And on that note…" Cassandra interrupted obviously amused, "a champagne toast for the bride. Please raise your glasses to salute my best friend on the occasion of her wedding. I wish you and Matt a long and happy life together. I love you, Liv!" Cassandra said as her eyes misted.

We raised our glasses filled with pink champagne. "To Olivia and Matt," we all said in unison.

"Hear, hear!" A loud voice rang out from the doorway of the dining room. All eyes turned to see who belonged to the booming voice.

"Mama?" Olivia yelped as a shocked look spread across her face. "What are you doing here?" I couldn't tell if Olivia was happily surprised or angry by the look that registered on her face. She seemed to be experiencing both emotions at the same time. I thought her reaction was strange.

"You didn't think I would miss my own daughter's bridal shower?" the bright red haired woman said sarcastically.

"Come here and give me a hug!" she demanded as Olivia rose from her chair hesitantly.

I could definitely see the family resemblance. Her mother was slightly taller than Olivia and had the same cat shaped eyes. She was wearing a lime green and white polka dot sheath dress with a button up front and coordinating belt. Her hair was piled high upon her head and held in place with a matching fabric head wrap. She was a very attractive lady.

"Glory be! What have you done to your hair? It looks awful like a cat licked it!" her mother commented as she ran her fingers through her daughter's hair and carefully analyzed it. Olivia stepped back to avoid any further inspection. Her face had turned red as if she were embarrassed. Everyone stopped speaking as if shocked by the unflattering remark.

I wondered to myself what would make someone say something so discouraging? Olivia looked radiant and her hair was most becoming. She had the type of red hair that couldn't be obtained from a hair salon, naturally curly and such a gorgeous red! Some mothers can tear down their daughter's self-esteem. I was beginning to understand why Olivia had not visited with her mother very often. I had sensed over the years of our friendship there was an unspoken tension between them. Now I was beginning to understand why.

"Ruby, why must you say something like that?" an older gray-haired lady chastised Olivia's mother. "This is her special day. Let her enjoy herself and quit being so critical."

"Hello, Grandma," Olivia said warmly embracing the diminutive lady. She smoothed the loose tendrils of hair away from her somber face and tried her best to compose herself.

"Well aren't you going to invite us in?" Ruby Rivers demanded. "Why I didn't drive all the way from Tullahoma to eat at McDonald's! I'm half-starved!"

"Come in, come in, Ladies!" Dixie stood up to greet them. "Please come in. We're so glad you could make it. Are there any more *unexpected* family members arriving?" She smiled insincerely at the two newcomers as she looked at her watch to make a point. Her meaning was not lost on me and it was not lost on Ruby. It was obvious Dixie didn't like being caught off guard with attendees who had not sent their RSVPs. She was publically spanking Ruby for not following proper etiquette and interrupting the shower.

"Cool your jets, Martha Stewart! I've just finished ratting and teasing ten senior citizens' hair for their weekly wash and set and rushed over the mountains to get here for my only daughter's wedding shower! "

Dixie caught her breath and placed her hand on her chest, obviously taken aback by Ruby's forthright comments. "Well, I never!" she stated and retreated back to her seat.

"Mama, please don't start anything today," Olivia pleaded. "Can't we enjoy a nice afternoon? Dixie didn't mean anything by what she said."

You could have heard a pin drop in the room as the guests looked quizzically at each other, not really sure what they had witnessed.

"I always set an extra table just in case," Sarah rushed forward to diffuse the situation. "I hope you ladies will take a seat and Gretchen and Emily will be right out with your tea and scones." The two ladies quietly made their way to their table and sat down.

"Would you like some tea?" I offered. "The apple Ceylon

is heavenly. I think you will really enjoy this," I said diplomatically as I filled their tea cups and tried to act as a distractor. Gretchen rushed in with a silver plated basket filled with scones and placed it in front of the newcomers.

"Thank you," Olivia's grandmother smiled genuinely at me. She seemed to be a bit embarrassed by her daughter-in-law's emotional outburst.

"Everyone, this is my mother, Ruby Rivers and my grandmother, Laurel Rivers," Olivia announced to the room as she took her seat again.

"So nice you could make it," Cassandra approached the twosome and politely extended her hand. "I'm Cassandra Reynolds. I've heard so much about both of you and I'm glad to finally meet you!"

"Oh, you're the one with the rich husband, right?" Ruby probed.

"Mother, that's inappropriate!" Olivia warned through gritted teeth. "We don't comment about people's finances." She glared at her mother, daring her to speak another word.

"Well, the papers reported her company was worth thirty million dollars. It can't be too personal if it was in the news. What's the big deal? If I had thirty million dollars, I would be crowing like a cock at sunrise!" she laughed as she took a bite of her scone.

Her running commentary reminded me of my own family member who didn't seem to have a filter from her brain to her mouth, my Aunt Imogene, who thankfully was too busy texting to say much right now. She had on more than one occasion given her opinion to my utter horror. Every family had one!

"Don't worry, Liv, its fine," Cassandra leaned over and whispered to her friend. Enjoy today."

"I'm trying my darndest!" Olivia forced an insincere smile and looked at me over her tea cup. "Sarah has really outdone herself with today's menu. Everything has been scrumptious!"

"Yes it has. This is the perfect place to have a bridal tea. Don't you think, Laurel?" I asked trying to include Olivia's grandmother in the conversation. I didn't want her to feel alienated sitting at the other table. "Would you care for more tea?"

"I'm fine thank you. This home is quite beautiful. I think it makes the perfect tea room," her grandmother smiled as she answered me. She was a definite contrast to Ruby's outspoken nature.

"I'm sure this house cost a pretty penny! I'm not sure I would feel comfortable living in something so refined. It's not my taste at all!" Ruby spoke aloud as she stopped long enough to loudly slurp her tea.

"It doesn't matter if this is your taste or not," Olivia said as she bristled at her mother's unending commentary. "Sarah has done a beautiful job decorating for *my* bridal shower. If you don't mind, let's keep opinions about taste to ourselves," she told rather than suggested to her mother.

"Sounds good to me," Dixie agreed as she stood up. "We have approximately five minutes before the savory course, so why don't we have the bride open one of her gifts, shall we?" she said as she glanced at her diamond encrusted Rolex.

"I would like her to begin with mine!" Cassandra said as she picked up a large wrapped box from the buffet table. Bet you can't guess what this is?" she said enthusiastically as she pushed her gift into Olivia's hands.

Olivia smiled as she eagerly began tearing the wrapping paper. She lifted the lid and exclaimed with excitement, "Oh, Cassandra! Thank you!"

"It's not that tacky equestrian china pattern you registered for at the Macy's is it? Why would anyone pay that much for Wedgewood china when you could have my pattern?" Ruby cackled as Olivia pulled out a tea pot with a beautiful equestrian scene on the side.

"Mother, please. It's beautiful, Cassandra. I love it! Thank you." Olivia stood up and hugged her platinum blonde friend.

"Everyone has a right to their own opinion. Why do you have to be so sensitive?" Ruby countered.

"Mother, I'm not being sensitive. I already explained to you why I didn't register for your china pattern. I wanted one of my own and one I happen to love that reflects who I am," she persisted.

"Okay, let's have the bride open another gift! Oh, look at this gorgeous paper!" Dixie squealed as she did her best to keep the shower moving in a positive direction.

"That gift is from me," Imogene spoke up between spoonfuls of her butternut squash soup. "I hope you and Lincoln enjoy it," she said with a mischievous gleam in her eye.

"Oh dear, it's probably edible panties," Lucy murmured loudly enough for all to hear. That got the room laughing and broke up some of the mother-daughter tension.

"Close, but no prize," Imogene laughed.

"Oh, Imogene, it's gorgeous!" Olivia remarked as she pulled a beautiful deep green velvet robe from the gift box. It matched her emerald and diamond engagement ring perfectly.

"There's more," Imogene told her as she watched a delighted Olivia.

"And a matching silk night gown? Oh, that's too much! Oh, thank you!" she stood up and went over to kiss Imogene on the cheek.

"Now I will be waiting to hear that these have worked some magic and you and that handsome detective will be expecting shortly. You two will make beautiful children!"

"I'm packing these for the honeymoon. Thank you Imogene!" Olivia beamed with happiness.

"Open mine next," Sarah said presenting Olivia with a burgundy covered package tied with an ornate gold bow. "I hope you like it!"

"I'm sure I will. Thank you, Sarah," Olivia said as she carefully pushed the ribbon off the box and took off the lid. "Oh, it's a collection of Jane Austin books. How thoughtful!"

"Lincoln reminds me of Mr. Darcy and you remind me of Elizabeth Bennett. Every time I read *Pride and Prejudice* I think of you two," she explained as she pushed her glasses back on the bridge of her nose.

"That is the sweetest thing you could ever say to me. Thank you," she sighed and gave Sarah a quick hug.

"I hope you won't be packing those books for your trip. That would definitely make for a dull honeymoon," Ruby snickered.

"Oh, they weren't meant for the honeymoon. I thought Olivia would enjoy reading them and having them in her library," Sarah stammered.

"They are lovely Sarah and I will cherish them. What is wrong with you, mother?" Olivia whispered in muted tones. "You have managed in a matter of minutes to be rude to every one of my friends." She turned back towards her guests. "Excuse me, everyone. I need a breath of fresh air," Olivia apologized as she pushed her chair back and hurried out of the room.

"I'll go check on her," Sarah said as she followed after her.

"Well! You've broken cardinal rule number one. Never upset the bride!" Dixie confronted Ruby with both hands on her hips. "I don't need any more shenanigans ruining this week. We have a lot of activities planned and I expect *everyone* to behave!"

"Who are you again?" Ruby narrowed her eyes as she looked Dixie over from head to toe.

"I'm Dixie Beauregard, event planner to the stars," Dixie said as she straightened her back and threw her head back defiantly.

"Well, Dixie Beauregard, event planner to the stars. I'm Ruby Rivers, mother of the bride. And I'm about to send you 'to the moon, Alice!'" Ruby said as she stood up from her seat and mimicked Jackie Gleason's iconic line.

"Let's all take a deep breath and calm down," Cassandra said jumping between the two women. "Mrs. Rivers, I'm sure you realize that this is a very stressful week for your daughter. She and Matt have been so busy planning and working on this wedding. We've all got to pull together right now and think of Olivia and what's best for her," Cassandra said in her most authoritative boardroom voice.

"I think I know what's best for my daughter. And I will not be lectured by some picnic blanket wearing, two-bit wedding planner," she said hatefully looking over Cassandra's shoulder at Dixie who was utterly unable to speak.

"Ruby, get a hold of yourself and start acting like a lady!" Laurel ordered pulling her daughter-in-law's arm. "You're acting like a fool!"

"I'll have you know this cape is from the Burberry fall collection. How dare you insult me like that! Who do you think you are? I have personally planned celebrity weddings from Tom Cruise to Jennifer Lopez and I will not tolerate being spoken to in such an insulting manner!" Dixie spouted.

"Well, that explains a lot!" Ruby lobbed a final insult.

"That's it; it's either her or me!" Dixie said firmly turning towards Cassandra.

"Everyone calm down and start acting like adults," Cassandra warned. "Stop this incessant bickering before you ruin Olivia's shower."

"Too late. The wedding is off," Sarah announced to the room. "Olivia's called the whole thing off!"

THREE

"Shane, you better get Lincoln over here on the double. She's called the wedding off!" I sputtered into my cell phone.

"What? What are you talking about?" he asked alarmed. "Slow down and give me details."

"Is Lincoln with you?" I continued.

"Yes. We're in Knoxville at McGhee Tyson airport picking up his brother and parents. What do you want me to do?"

"Let me think about this. It won't do any good to tell him right now. It will only upset everyone and Olivia has been known to change her mind. Just don't say a word about this to him right now," I thought aloud.

"Tell me what happened. I thought she was really looking forward to her bridal shower today," he said sadly.

"She was until her mother showed up and began hurling insults at everyone. It was terrible, Shane! That woman has anger management issues. Dixie has threatened to quit, Olivia is upstairs with Sarah crying her eyes out and I'm downstairs trying to maintain some semblance of normality and keep the gossip at a low if I can keep Aunt Imogene off her Twitter account," I explained.

I had removed myself from the dining room and gone back into the kitchen where I could speak privately to Shane.

Gretchen and Emily were keeping smiles on their faces and tea cups full while we hoped Olivia and her mom would patch things up and call a truce. Hopefully we could resume the party if everyone would behave.

"Well tonight is the big dinner where the Rivers and the Lincolns meet. What do you want me to do? I feel like Matt needs to know what's going on. His parents' flight just arrived at the gate," Shane informed me.

"Don't say anything for now. I'll work some magic on my end and we'll just keep this quiet. I'm sure Olivia will calm down before the dinner tonight. I think what would be best is giving a crash course in decorum and manners to Ruby Rivers. She's a piece of work!" I reported.

"And we wonder where our fiery redhead gets it from!" Shane joked.

"She may have red hair, often voices her opinion and is known to be fiery, but she is not hurtful like her mother. There's definitely a history there. Now I understand better why Olivia has tried to keep her mother from visiting Dogwood Cove. She may be a deal breaker!" I said truthfully.

"I'll keep the Lincolns entertained and as far as I know, everything is set for the dinner tonight at the General Morgan Inn. My lips are sealed. I'll call you after I get everyone to the hotel," he said as we exchanged goodbyes.

"Amelia, dear. Someone has to talk some sense into that woman," Imogene said shaking her head. "She's destructive! I can't believe she just shows up and has everyone upset. What is the matter with her?"

I had to hide my amusement at Imogene's remark since my aunt was known about town for offering her opinion, solicited or not.

"It's her need for attention," Laurel Rivers spoke up as she entered the kitchen. "I want to apologize. I knew Ruby was wound up today, but this is totally uncalled for. I know you girls have worked hard to make today special for my Olivia and I'm truly sorry," she softly said placing her hands together. It was apparent that she was quite sad at what had transpired this afternoon.

"There's some tension between them and quite a history, I take it," I said to Laurel. "I knew Olivia didn't talk much about her mom and they didn't visit often, but I had no idea the problems were so severe."

"Ruby is lonely right now. My son, Olivia's father Christopher, died about two years ago. Ruby hasn't been herself since then. Christopher was the buffer between those two headstrong women and without him around, there hasn't been any peace between them," she sadly disclosed.

"I knew Olivia was close to her dad. She talked about him all the time. She told me that Lincoln reminds her of him in so many ways. I'm hoping that Ruby and Olivia can patch things up before this evening. The Lincolns just arrived at the airport and they are on their way to the General Morgan Inn to check in and get ready for dinner this evening," I enlightened Laurel.

"Let me talk to her. We've always been so close. Maybe I can fix this problem. Will you take me to Olivia?" Laurel pleaded with tears in her blue eyes. "Christopher would be so upset if he knew what had happened today."

"What about Ruby? Anyone talking some sense into her?" Imogene spoke up. "It won't matter if you smooth things over with Olivia if her mother keeps the attacks going. I don't know too many people who wouldn't tell her to leave!"

"I've already spoken with Ruby. She is in the front room with Cassandra composing herself. She has promised me that she will behave. If you will take me to Olivia, I will make things right with my family."

"Grandma Laurel, I believe you will," I said hugging her. Follow me up the back stairs and I'll take you to Olivia. Be careful, these steps are steep."

"I take Zumba. I'm pretty agile. I'll be fine, dear," she said lightly.

Laurel and I mounted the stairs and arrived at the second floor landing. Antique barrister bookcases lined the walls and were filled with Sarah's collection of classics. Everything from *Wuthering Heights* to *The Scarlet Letter* was contained behind the beveled glass doors. She had done a brilliant job of finding antiques that suited her eclectic style. Everything was in good taste and I could see Sarah's personality in each carefully selected piece.

We walked down the hall to Sarah's library and I quietly knocked and waited for a response before I pushed the solid oak door open.

"Who is it?" Sarah asked quietly.

"It's Amelia and Grandma Laurel," I replied. There was a slight pause followed by the door being opened by Sarah. A tear streaked face greeted us as we walked into the comfortable room filled with a large mossy green velvet sofa and oversized chairs. A flowered antique needlepoint rug was the centerpiece of the room and tied the muted tones of sage, burnt umber and cream together. It was a very serene and calming room and I hoped it would have that effect on our bride.

"Is mama with you?" Olivia asked wiping her nose. "I don't want to talk to her right now."

"She's downstairs. I've already spoken with her and you have my word she will not be any more trouble to you," Grandma Laurel said moving Olivia's legs and taking a seat on the sofa next to her. "You've got to quit this carrying on and go downstairs. You still have guests to look after," she reminded her.

"Grandma, why is she so hateful? I've tried to figure her out and I just can't understand her! I purposefully have kept her from meeting Lincoln because I just knew something would happen. I would rather elope than go through all this!" she said crying and blowing her nose.

"Olivia, your mother is a difficult woman to understand. I know that she's hurting right now and lashing out at everyone. She misses your Dad and she's angry that you have been pushing her away," Laurel informed her.

"I'm pushing her away? I'm pushing her away? How can I possibly be close or let my guard down around someone who constantly criticizes me? If it's not my hair, it's my makeup, my profession, it's always something. I have pushed her away because for years she has made me feel like I've never been good enough!" she admitted and began sobbing on her grandmother's shoulder.

Sarah and I exchanged glances and turned back to face our friend. I felt like we were intruding on the conversation, but I was also worried that Olivia would still cancel the wedding if I didn't stay and intervene.

"Let me get you a cup of tea, Olivia," Sarah volunteered and left the room, closing the door quietly behind her.

"Olivia, your mother needs you more than ever now. You

are all that she has and yes, I understand her constant criticism is hurtful. But have you made her feel included in your life? Do you invite her to come visit your ranch? Do you call her up just to talk?" Laurel pointed out. "She feels cut out ever since your Dad died and probably before then.

Olivia raised her head and looked at her grandmother puzzled.

"It was always you and Christopher. You were the apple of his eye. His little spitfire girl, a small version of Ruby. And he loved you with all of his heart. Once you came along, Ruby was somewhat pushed to the side. I don't think Christopher meant to, but his whole world revolved around you and Ruby didn't feel included," she continued.

"When Christopher was tragically taken from us too young, the divide between you and your mother just widened. She wasn't going to let you in and you were not going to let her in. The pain was just too intense and you both have been grieving in your own way. If you two hardheads would just see that, I think you could have a new beginning, don't you sweetheart?" Laurel said patting Olivia's hand.

"Grandma, I love you!" Olivia said shakily. "Matt Lincoln is the most wonderful man I have ever met. If Mama keeps criticizing and picking at me one of two things will happen. Matt will listen to her and believe what she says or he will see me get upset and decide he's done with me. I won't lose him because of her. I think it's best to keep my distance."

"Only you can decide what is best for you. I can only tell you what I think. I've known you your whole life and your mother for thirty-five years. I love you both dearly, but this bickering has got to end. If you make a decision to cut your mother out of your wedding, you will regret it. I know about regret and it's a bitter pill to swallow. Before you decide what you are going to do, think about what I said, will you dear?" Laurel cupped her granddaughter's chin and looked into Olivia's eyes. She gently smoothed her hair and kissed her cheek.

Sarah arrived with a pot of tea and four tea cups. She carefully poured and handed each of us a cup. I sat down in one of the chairs and did my best to smile hopefully at Olivia.

"Look, Liv. All mothers and daughters lock horns. Its part of the circle of becoming a woman. You have worked so hard to plan this wedding. Don't let this ruin it. I think Laurel is right. Your mom is acting out because she is hurt," I rationalized. "Be the bigger person here and make up with your mother."

"This is just what I didn't want to happen. I was afraid she would do something to cast a negative vibe on my wedding," Olivia sniffed and took a sip of her tea.

"Only if you let her," Sarah observed.

"If I let her? What do you mean?" Olivia paused and looked at her friend.

"Only if you let her. You have control of your reactions and your emotions. Don't give her the power," she advised. "You and only you can decide if you will allow her to upset you."

"What are you talking about? Is this some kind of new-age garbage you've been reading about?" Olivia accused.

"No, something I try to live. Life is unpredictable. We can react to what is thrown in our path in a positive or negative way. I choose positive," Sarah calmly stated.

"So you're saying I'm negative, is that it?" Olivia said pulling herself up straight.

"No. I'm saying handle your mom in a positive way. When she begins to say something negative, channel your energy into talking about something positive. You would be surprised at the result if you don't allow her to steer the conversation. You can keep her on a more positive path," Sarah smiled and placed her hands in her lap.

"Have you tried talking to that woman? How in the world do I respond in a positive way when she announces to the room that my hair looks like the cat got a hold of it? What do you suggest oh 'wise guru of positivity?'" Olivia asked sarcastically.

"Well, your mom is a hairdresser, right?" Sarah asked.

"Yeah. So?" Olivia questioned mockingly.

"Why not ask her to fix your hair?" Sarah stated.

"Are you crazy? Have you seen the beehives she fixes for the ladies at the senior citizen center?" Olivia retorted. "I would wind up looking like a member of the B52's!"

"Maybe temporarily, but what could it hurt? It might make your mom feel really good that you allowed her to do something nice for you," she countered.

"What will I accomplish by looking like the *Bride of Frankenstein?*" she argued stubbornly.

"An upsweep is temporary. What can it hurt? You simply take out the bobby pins and wash out the hairspray. Nothing ventured, nothing gained!" Sarah laughed. "But it will make your mom feel included by allowing her to do something nice for you."

"I see your point, Sarah. I know you wouldn't care to have a beehive with some of the outfits I've seen you wear, no offense, but I on the other hand would rather not be seen in public like that."

Olivia was referring to Sarah's penchant for wearing themed outfits. Sometimes it was a Japanese Kimono, other times an Audrey Hepburn inspired *Breakfast at Tiffany's* up-sweep and black dress. She enjoyed experimenting with different looks and had fun doing it.

"Do you hear yourself, Liv? You're just as stubborn as your mother!" Laurel fussed at her granddaughter. "Sarah is right. Give a little, take a little. But start somewhere!"

"I will, I will! I'm just a little wound up right now with all the wedding plans. I've got a lot on my mind," she admitted.

"Speaking of wedding plans, the Lincolns have arrived in Knoxville. Shane and Matt have picked them up and they are on their way to the General Morgan Inn. You have dinner plans in just two hours," I reminded her.

"Oh gosh! Look at me! I'm a wreck!" Olivia cried out. "I'm sure I look like a puffer fish with my eyes all swollen. What am I going to do?"

"I can take care of that," Ruby Rivers said walking into the room. "Sarah, have you got any more cucumbers?"

"I sure do! I'll get a few slices. Good thinking!" she said and scurried down the hall.

"Look, I'm sorry, Olivia. I don't know what's wrong with me," Ruby said tenderly. "I didn't mean to ruin your shower. I'm so sorry. Will you forgive me?"

"Sure Mama. I'm sorry too. I shouldn't have been so upset," she compromised. They walked towards each other and gave a long embrace.

"Now, let's do something about your hair. Anyone have hairspray and a curling iron on them by chance?" Ruby inquired.

"Oh, I'm sure Sarah does," I laughed and answered.

"What about all the guests downstairs? I feel so bad about walking out!" Olivia moaned.

"Gretchen is serving the savory course and they are all eating and enjoying themselves. Aunt Imogene is entertaining them with her latest story. Let's focus on getting you to the dinner on time," I suggested.

"That sounds good! Any chance I could have a couple of those cucumber sandwiches and quiche?" Olivia asked.

Well that was one meltdown averted. Olivia's appetite was back and family harmony restored. Let's hope the rest of the wedding week would go better!

FOUR

The General Morgan Inn was an historic landmark in our area and was the perfect backdrop for the Lincolns and Rivers to meet. The hotel had been welcoming guests since 1854 and was a favorite spot for weddings, business affairs or an overnight stay in one of its fifty-one well-appointed rooms. Olivia had requested that Shane and I join the group this evening to act as a buffer in case Ruby decided to act up again. After the bridal tea, I knew I had my work cut out.

Shane had remained at the General Morgan after he got the Lincolns settled into their hotel rooms. He was waiting in the lobby when I arrived with Olivia, Laurel and Ruby.

"Olivia, you look stunning! You've done something different with your hair!" he complimented her as he spun her around.

"Thanks for noticing, Shane. My mother gets all the credit tonight," Olivia smiled and acknowledged Ruby who was glowing under the praise.

"We just had to do an upsweep to show off those beautiful emerald earrings Matt gave her for a wedding gift. Doesn't she look like a porcelain doll?" Ruby raved. "Wait until he sees her. His jaw will drop."

"Mama, you're embarrassing me," Olivia sheepishly grinned under the scrutiny. "I do hope he likes my outfit. Cassandra selected it for tonight."

Olivia did look like a million bucks from her sea foam green velvet trousers to her matching silk chemise. The color was perfect for her fair complexion and ginger hair which Ruby had expertly fixed in a French twist. Her eyes were sparkling. Yes, Matt's jaw was going to drop.

"And least I not forget my darling," Shane said bestowing a kiss on my lips. "You look gorgeous. Good choice," he said raising his eyebrows up and down and giving me a wicked grin. He had helped me select my halter dress in a deep plum shade. The plunging back of the dress was a bit of a departure from my conservative wardrobe, but I was pleased to see his reaction. He placed his hand at the small of my back and left it there. We had been married over sixteen years and I had never regretted one day with him.

"You two still have the fire in your relationship. I hope Lincoln and I are as lucky as you two," Olivia admitted wistfully.

"Here they come now," Shane said as the Lincolns approached our quartet. I hoped all would go well for this momentous meeting of the families for the first time.

"Olivia dear," Audrey Lincoln said as she bent towards Olivia to give her a warm hug. She stepped back and admired the petite beauty before her. "Matt, you do have a beautiful bride!" she said as she straightened her red suit jacket. Her salt and pepper streaked hair was perfectly coiffed reminding me of Mary Tyler Moore's infamous flip up style.

"Yes, I do mother," he agreed and gave a kiss on Olivia's lips. "Let me introduce everyone," he insisted. "Dad, mother, this is Olivia's mother, Ruby and her grandmother, Laurel."

"So very nice to meet you," Ruby said politely as she shook hands with the very slim and poised Audrey Lincoln.

"Oh, give me a hug! We're family after all," Laurel said as she warmly embraced Matt's towering father, Lewis. She looked like a munchkin wrapped in his burly arms.

"So nice to meet you both," Lewis chuckled and stepped back to shake hands with Ruby. He was wearing a navy blue sports jacket with brass buttons over his open collared buttondown.

"And this good-looking guy is my brother, Tom!" Matt said patting his younger sibling on the arm. "I'm going to have to keep a close eye on you so you don't try to steal my bride," he teased.

"No chance of that, Matt. Olivia only has eyes for you," Tom joked as he gave his future sister-in-law a squeeze. "Good to see you, Liv! It is nice to meet everyone." He was tall and muscular like Matt, but his coloring was more like his father's blonde hair and blue eyes.

"Why don't we get seated at our table," Matt suggested and led the way to Brumleys, the renowned restaurant inside The General Morgan Inn.

"What a lovely hotel. I'm so glad you suggested it," Audrey Lincoln remarked.

"Oh, thank Amelia. She is friends with the manager of the hotel," Olivia stated.

"They purchase their coffees and teas from our company," I explained to the Lincolns as we were guided to our table located in a dark paneled room. The candles and silverware gleamed on the crisp linen tablecloths and gave a warm glow to the historic room. Shane pulled out my chair and assisted

Laurel with hers. Her eyes crinkled at the corners as she smiled up at him.

"What is the name of your coffee business?" Audrey politely inquired.

"Smoky Mountain," Shane responded. "We're a fairly new business, but we have been growing quickly. "What line of work are you in, Lewis?"

"Banking," Lewis answered as our server passed around our menus. "I am in management with First Texas Banks," he continued as he placed his napkin in his lap.

"Must be interesting," Ruby joined in. I smiled as I mentally noted she was not making financial comments in front of the Lincolns. Maybe Laurel had talked some sense into her daughter-in-law after all!

"It's been interesting with the financial situation in our country lately, but that's enough talk about my business," he concluded. "How's work, Matt? Caught any cows roaming outside their fences?" he kidded, a reference to the small population of Dogwood Cove and the fact that cows outnumbered the citizens two to one.

"Not any today, Dad!" Matt answered light heartedly.

"What's good on the menu?" Tom inquired.

"I think the Oysters Rockefeller are superb as well as the rosemary lamb chops," I suggested. "Everything Brumleys serves is wonderful. I don't think you'll be disappointed."

"Tom, tell us about yourself," Ruby quietly spoke up. "Are you a police officer too?"

"No, I leave chasing the bad guys to Matt. I work with Dad at First Texas," he said.

"Tom is following in the old man's footsteps," Matt added.

"Something we planned on you doing as well," Audrey muttered as she gazed down at her menu. Did I detect a disapproving tone to her comment?

"Banking is not my idea of adventure, mother," Matt commented.

"And being shot at by criminals and putting your life on the line every day is?" she said with anxiety written all over her face. "I wish you would do something in the private sector and get out of police work entirely!"

"Well, I think I will be ordering the filet," Shane spoke up trying to break the tension.

"That sounds wonderful," I agreed. "What will you be having, Grandmother Laurel?"

"It all sounds good. But, I think I will try the tilapia tonight," she decided.

"So, how is the wedding coming along?" Lewis asked Olivia. "Anything we can do to help?"

"I'm glad just to have you here," Olivia responded. "Dixie has triple checked everything and as long as the weather holds for Saturday, everything is right on track," she concluded.

"Yes, Dixie gave me a checklist for what to pack," Audrey said flatly. "She said to bring boots and jeans for a trail ride, is that right?"

"Yes, I thought it would be fun to get everyone together for a trail ride around Riverbend Ranch. We're also going to have a bonfire and BBQ tomorrow evening for close friends and family."

"That sounds great!" Tom piped up. "I love horseback riding. We don't do too much of it in the big city."

"And what big city would that be?" Ruby asked as she broke off a piece of her roll.

"Dallas. Yeah, they don't have too many open places to ride anymore. You have to go more towards Ft. Worth or out west to really ride," he informed her.

"I've never been to Dallas. I'm sure it must be something to see!" Ruby spoke up.

"We had hoped that Olivia and Matt would be moving back home after the wedding, right Lewis?" Audrey mentioned.

"Mother, we've already discussed that and Olivia and I both have careers here in Dogwood Cove," Matt said authoritatively.

"Matthew, Dallas is where you grew up. You *had* a wonderful career as a detective with the police department. I still don't understand why you threw that all away to move here. What is the allure anyway? What could this town possibly offer that Dallas does not?" Audrey challenged her oldest son.

"Not again, mother. And please, not tonight. Let's enjoy getting to know the Rivers," he pleaded.

"Please, Audrey," Lewis patted his wife's hand. "Let's have a nice evening. Why don't you order a glass of wine and unwind a little?"

"What are you insinuating, Lewis? That I'm uptight? I do not need a glass of wine to unwind and I don't see anything wrong with asking my son a question about his future," she snapped.

"Oh heavens," Laurel murmured and rolled her eyes.

"Oh, here come the appetizers!" Olivia observed as Oyster Rockefeller and salmon croutes were brought to the table. "I'm famished. Let's dig in!"

"So we will be expecting you to visit Dallas during Christmas," Audrey pressed.

"We haven't made our holiday plans yet," Matt told her as he helped himself to an oyster. "Anyone else?" he passed the serving dish around.

"I assumed you would be spending *every* Christmas with us," Audrey said putting her fork down rather loudly. "We hardly see you!"

"Why would that be?" Ruby interjected. "Olivia has family in Tullahoma too, you know."

"Tulla what?" Audrey said sarcastically.

"Tullahoma is our hometown. I don't see why you would assume that they would always go to Dallas for Christmas," Ruby surmised.

"Mama, please. Let's not talk about this right now," Olivia begged.

"Why not?" Audrey shot back. "I think it would be good for both mothers to hear about our children's plans."

"This is why I'm single," Tom jested. "Mom would run off anyone I brought home!" he laughed as he buttered his roll.

"Been through that, bro!" Matt chuckled as the brothers knocked knuckles in a 'fist bump.'

"So Christmas is up in the air? What about Easter? We are a practicing Catholic family. We should be together during the high holidays," Audrey nagged.

"We haven't decided which church we will be attending," Matt told his mother.

"Which Catholic Church, that is what you are saying?" Audrey questioned. "I'm sure there is more than one in Dogwood Cove."

"No, mother, which church as in which denomination. Olivia was raised Southern Baptist. We are going to compromise and pick a church we are both comfortable attending," Matt said impatiently.

"Matthew Scott Lincoln, that is not an option," Audrey persisted. "You cannot undo generations of church tradition!"

"Audrey!" Lewis whispered loudly. "This is not the time and place to discuss their religious decisions. We're here to enjoy this time together and to get to know the Rivers better. Please eat and be quiet!"

"I did not raise my son to leave his faith and turn his back on his family. Really, Lewis! I would expect you to grow a backbone and talk to your son before he ruins the rest of his life!" she shouted.

"Remember when we had this conversation with my mother?" Lewis gently reminded his high-strung wife. "We compromised and I left the Methodist Church when we married."

"Excuse me?" Ruby Rivers leaned forward in her chair. She was not about to let Audrey's comment pass. "Ruin his life? Are you implying that marrying my daughter is ruining your son's life?"

"Disengage, mama. Disengage!" Olivia advised thru gritted teeth.

"I am not going to sit here and listen to 'miss cock-of-the-walk' go around blaming *you* for her son making up his own mind about his life! Have you ever thought maybe he moved to get away from his over-controlling mother?" Ruby snapped.

"Ruby, you have gone too far," Laurel tried to calm her daughter-in-law. "Please don't make things worse!"

"I don't think they could be much worse. The woman has basically insulted Olivia's hometown, her religion and has blamed her for Matt's decision to move. How can I not take up for my daughter? Someone has to!" she said defensively.

"I can take up for myself, mama! I am choosing not to argue tonight. This is *our wedding* after all! Excuse me, everyone!" Olivia said pushing her chair away from the table and getting up to leave the dining room. "I need to get some fresh air."

"I need to see to my bride!" Matt said as he threw down his napkin, glared at his mother and left to follow his fiancée.

"Oh, dear!" Laurel commented quietly next to me. "This has been a hard day for Olivia, hasn't it?"

"Yes it has, Laurel. You're right," I said worried about my friend. I was hoping everyone would make a peace pact to make it through the wedding week without another altercation. I wasn't so sure that all parties would be amicable to this agreement. Olivia and Matt's relationship would be put to the test in more ways than they could have imagined. I hoped they survived the invasion of the in-laws and would make it to the altar intact!

FIVE

"The ranch is looking great." I observed as I joined Olivia out in the barn. She was grooming Maggie May and had her cross-tied as she combed out her mane. "How are you holding up?"

She continued spraying fly repellent on Maggie's coat as she reached in her pocket to find a small apple to reward her prized mare. She looked at me and I could see the lack of sleep in her red-rimmed eyes. This was not a happy bride.

"I'm as well as can be expected with both Ruby and Audrey in the vicinity. Last night I begged Lincoln to run away and elope," she admitted.

"And what did he say?" I pried.

"He said we should be reasonable. We would be disappointing a lot of people who had traveled a long way to be with us on our wedding day. I'm starting to think it's just not worth the trouble," she revealed walking over to the grain bin and filling up a feed bucket. She hooked it inside the stall door and led Maggie May back to her area. She securely latched the paddock lock and Maggie could be heard contentedly munching her grain.

"How can I help ease some of the tension?" I asked sincerely.

"Keep those two women away from me," Olivia strongly replied, "and Dixie too! She's driving me nuts!"

"She's just doing her job, Liv! Don't be too hard on her," I recommended. "Where are the mothers anyway?"

"Lincoln is playing golf with his family over at the country club right now. That should take up most of the morning. They're going to grab lunch there before they head over for the trail ride this afternoon. Mama is with Cassandra shopping in town. Hopefully that will take a while."

"Did you fill Cassandra in on what happened last night?" I asked.

"Yeah and she's doing some shopping intervention to help me out. She's going to take Mama and Grandma Laurel to the Pink Dogwood for lunch afterwards. Cassandra has a way with people. It probably comes from her negotiation skills in the boardroom at Reynolds."

"So you get a little break from everyone. That's good," I told her as I put my arm around her and gave her a comforting sqeeze. "Why don't you go soak in the tub and take a long bubble bath," I suggested.

"That sounds heavenly, but I have to get the bonfire ready and the tables set up for the BBQ. Dixie has given me quite a list of things to do."

"Well, from the aroma coming from your smokers, everything is going to taste wonderful tonight. Sarah has baked a mess of her cornbread, and made potato salad and her famous five bean baked beans. I've brought my Meyer lemon and chamomile tea meringue pies and our latest iced tea blend. Cassandra is bringing the Mojitos. It's going to be a fun afternoon and evening."

"Fun for whom? I've got to find a way to keep those two alpha females as far apart as possible. Now you understand why Lincoln and I don't live near our parents," she confessed.

I had a pretty good grasp of the situation. Olivia's mother had been hard on her growing up. It appeared as if Lincoln couldn't please his mother either. Being independent, in my opinion, was probably best for the two of them.

"Shane's mom gave me a hard time when we were first married. She was so competitive over recipes and whose cooking was better. When I stopped caring so much and became interested in having her teach me some of her special traditions and recipes, she backed off. I think she just wanted to know that she was still important to him even though he was married. She didn't want to be replaced," I speculated.

"I can see that would be hard for a mother," Olivia conceded. "But to dictate your religion and holiday schedule, that's much different than being competitive over cooking."

"What does Lincoln say?" I probed.

"He told me not to worry. His mother has been trying to run his life since he was in diapers. He does his best to ignore her comments. I'm not so good at doing that," Olivia said.

"Let him handle his mom and you handle yours. That way you don't step on each other's toes and cause any hurt feelings. He loves you, Liv!"

"OK, I've got Dan setting up the hay bales around the bonfire area," Dixie expertly reported as she entered the barn. She was wearing quite a costume—a white fringed leather jacket, matching white studded boots and skin tight designer jeans. "You're going to load up the long tables and bring them down to the pasture in twenty minutes, right?" she told Olivia.

"Yes, Broom Hilda! I've already got them loaded in my pickup," she snarled.

"Look, after your mother's antics yesterday, you're lucky I'm still here. But I am a professional after all and Cassandra and Doug Reynolds are some of my best repeat clients. I stayed on as personal favor to them, but I won't tolerate any name calling!" Dixie informed her as she adjusted her white cowboy hat.

"You look like a professional all right. A professional rodeo clown in your *Lone Ranger* themed costume," Olivia muttered under her breath. Only I could overhear what she was saying.

"And we're so glad you decided to stay on," I interceded. "This wedding is going to be the talk of the town! Dixie, you have outdone yourself!"

"I hope the bride shares your sentiments," Dixie said haughtily. "I would hate to think of what would happen to this wedding if I were not around to see to every painstaking detail."

"It's going to be quite a lovely event despite you," Olivia snapped. "You're the one whose grand scheme of a ranch wedding looked like a bad episode of *Hee Haw* with scare crows, overalls and corn cob pipes. This wedding has been *my* vision from the beginning."

"Ladies, ladies, let's keep our tempers in check," I recommended. "Everyone has worked very hard to make the ranch beautiful for Saturday. Let's not ruin everything by arguing. Nerves are running high right now, that's all!" I said trying to put a positive spin on the near disastrous throwdown brewing between the two.

"I've got too much to deal with now to even address your comments. I'm going to take the high road and move on!" Dixie declared sashaying quickly out of the barn. She was met by several of her "Dixie's Pixies" who were waiting to fulfill every command she barked.

"I'll tell you what road she can take. How about highway to …"

"Let it go, Liv!" I advised. "Look at her poor staff. They are running around with those earbuds and radios like they are secret service. I can't believe she insists on her people wearing head-to-toe black."

"Have you heard her snap at that blonde guy, Austin? I feel sorry for him. She's really been riding his case this week," Olivia empathized. "The poor guy has to fetch her fat-free caramel lattes with soy milk, mind you, chauffeur her around in her pimped out Land Rover, and be her walking Rolodex. She barks orders to him non-stop!"

"Yes, I've noticed she is a high maintenance employer. I guess that's what it takes to make it as a top event planner in Hollywood," I speculated.

"Have you seen Dixie?" a very thin "pixie" with jet-black spiked hair asked as she stepped into the barn.

"She left about two minutes ago. She was headed to the corral," Olivia advised the almost emaciated young lady. "Can I help with anything?"

"No, just hit a snafu with the bluegrass band. The lead fiddle player is out with the flu," she informed us. "No worries, we'll find a replacement group."

"Call East Tennessee State University," I suggested. "They have a bluegrass department and an award winning band. I'm sure they would be happy to do the event."

"Thanks, Mrs. Spencer!" the young lady smiled as she skipped out of the barn. "You just saved my hide," she shouted over her shoulder as she waved goodbye.

"I bet she would have been royally chewed out for that," Olivia commented. "Good save Amelia!"

"I did many events at the tea room and hosted many weddings. I'm an old pro when it comes to this," I laughed.

"I should have asked you to handle it. You know me so well, it wouldn't have been a constant battle to have the wedding reflect my style and preferences," Olivia sighed.

"What can I do to help? I'm here early to lend a hand. Put me to work," I volunteered.

"Ride with me to the corral. I'm going to deliver these tables before Dixie blows a gasket because I'm not on time according to her schedule. Then you can help me bring the horses down for the trail ride," she thought aloud.

"I'd be happy to do it!"

We rode down the graveled driveway to the bottom of the property where things were in high gear for tonight's BBQ. Olivia was right. Dixie did have her worker bees running everywhere, stacking wood for the bonfire, sweeping off the picnic area for the dinner and stringing large white lights in the trees. It was going to be a very festive evening from what I could tell.

Dan and a few of the other farmhands unloaded the long rectangular tables from the back of Olivia's forest green F350 pickup. Though she was a little lady, she enjoyed the power behind her large truck. It was perfect for hauling horse trailers and carrying large loads. She needed it with all her farm duties.

"Thanks Dan! Tell Carl and Bill to head up to the house. I've got lunch ready and I'm sure you've worked up quite an appetite. I know I have!" Olivia yelled to her foreman as she drove up the steep hill back to her farm house. It was situated next to the Tennessee River and had quite a breathtaking view of the surrounding mountains that nestled Dogwood Cove in a secure valley.

We headed inside and Olivia began creating 'Dagwood' sandwiches for the ranch hands. She piled cold cuts, assorted cheeses, bread and butter pickles, sliced tomatoes, and red onions on large hoagie rolls slathered in mayonnaise and Dijon mustard. She mounded pasta salad and bunches of grapes on the side. It would fill up a hungry cowboy!

After washing up at the outdoor sink, the ranch hands took a seat at the long trestle table on the back porch. Olivia often entertained outside and had installed a full kitchen overlooking the rushing river. I brought out a tray loaded down with lemonade and bottled water for the thirsty and hardworking fellas.

"I've made extra sandwiches, so everybody eat up," Olivia said with satisfaction. She grabbed a plate for both of us as we joined the men at the table. It was like a working family at Riverbend Ranch. Everyone was an intricate part of the running of the ranch and had their assigned duties. Lunch breaks were eagerly anticipated.

"She been working you hard, Dan?" Olivia asked the foreman between bites of her sandwich. "I hear she's been running you ragged."

"Can't complain, but I'll be glad when it's over," he admitted. The rest of the guys laughed and continued eating. Dan was a man of few words. His statement or lack there-of, spoke volumes to me.

"You let me know if she gets out of hand," Olivia told him. "I mean it, Dan. You will tell me if I need to speak with her!"

"Aw, she's all right. Just a little high-strung," he said nonchalantly.

"Dan. Dan. Hawkeye to Dan," a voice on a static filled channel interrupted the lunch.

"What the heck? 'Hawkeye?'" Olivia inquired.

"Dan to Hawkeye," Dan said into a walkie-talkie.

"Need you down at the corral, ASAP, over!" Dixie commanded.

"Is that Dixie?" Olivia questioned. "Give me that, Dan!" She grabbed the radio out of the surprised foreman's hand. He shook his head and grinned. The other ranch hands sat back and watched the scene with amusement.

"Hawkeye, this is *Bridezilla!* Dan and the guys are taking their lunch break. Over!" Olivia shouted into the radio.

"I need them to level the driveway before our guests arrive. Wrap up lunch, over!" Dixie ordered.

"Ah, Hawkeye, my guys need to finish their lunch. They will be down in fifteen minutes and that's the final word, over!" Olivia replied.

Dan shook his head and looked around the table. He kept eating and didn't comment on the conversation. He wiped his mouth with a napkin and grinned at the farmhands.

"That settles that!" Olivia said to the group. Please go get another sandwich and eat up. The trail ride will take up a lot of your energy. But please stick around for the BBQ tonight.

I hope you remembered to ask your wives and girlfriends to come join us. There will be plenty of food," Olivia offered.

We were all looking forward to tonight's BBQ. Olivia was serving mesquite beef brisket in honor of her groom's Texan roots. The beef was from her herd at Riverbend Ranch.

She was very generous with the guys. They all had been with her a long time and they were a family. Each person had been carefully chosen for their care for the animals, skill at ranching and their unwavering help with the children who took lessons. They had helped Olivia build her business and would have not missed her wedding for the world.

"We better get on back before Miss Dixie gets too perturbed. Thanks for lunch, Olivia," Dan said putting his cowboy hat back on. "See you Amelia!" he nodded and walked over to the truck.

"Here, boys. Take these extra sandwiches and drinks with you. Don't let her boss you too much," she advised.

"We're fine. She's temporary," Dan answered.

"Thanks Olivia for lunch," Carl and Bill waved as the truck kicked up dust and drove down the long driveway.

"That woman! I could just kill her!" Olivia threatened.

"Let's baste the beef and check the smokers," I suggested. "We've got a BBQ and trail ride to look forward to."

We started clearing plates and taking them inside. That would be one of the last routine tasks we performed before Olivia's world would be turned upside down.

SIX

*B*ack at the barn, Olivia, Dan and the ranch hands worked to saddle up the horses for the trail ride. The guests had not yet arrived, but the horses were in the corral, ready to go. It would just be a matter of matching the riders to their steeds.

"Dixie's Pixies" flowed in and out of the barn, asking their diva questions and reporting for duty. They were transforming the inside of the barn into a festive reception area. Currently six "pixies" were in the hayloft area wrapping white lights around each of the rafters, creating a soft lighting effect for the event.

"Don't go near that stall," Olivia warned one of the "Pixies." "Apple Jack is missing an eye and he tends to be jumpy. Just leave him alone and he won't bother you," she cautioned.

"Sorry. I didn't know," the ponytailed worker said jumping out of the way. "I'll just start the lights over here," she said as Apple Jack nipped at her.

"Quit that Jack," Olivia said clutching the horse's bridle. "You are being hateful today," she continued, soothing the high-spirited horse by rubbing his forelock and face. "There, there. All this commotion has spooked you. I think it would be best to leave you in the barn and not take you on the trail ride."

"Carl, would you keep an eye on everyone in the barn?" Olivia asked the tall man. "All this activity is spooking the horses. I don't want someone getting hurt," she warned.

"Sure will," Carl said as he filled water buckets and began mucking the stalls.

"Amelia, will you take Maggie and Max down to the corral?" Olivia requested.

"Sure. No problem," I said grabbing their lead ropes.

"I'll follow with Annie and Willow," she said making a gentle clucking noise to her pair of horses.

"It's the perfect day to ride," I said as I looked up and enjoyed the sunshine breaking through overhead trees. The leaves were brilliant in hues of gold, burnt orange, bright red and brown. This was my favorite time of year and the perfect backdrop for Olivia's wedding.

"It's good weather. I hope the rest of the week holds out as well," she said hopefully.

"Does your mom ride?" I inquired.

"She used to, but she's decided to stay at the house with Grandma instead of going on the ride this afternoon. She'll probably be worn out from shopping with Cassandra," Olivia laughed. "I've already heard from Sarah that they had a nice lunch at the tea room and are headed over here now."

"Oh that's good. Maybe she will stay in good spirits today!" I said as I slowly walked the mares down the steep driveway. They were used to the incline and had a much better footing than I did at the moment.

"Does Lincoln's family ride too?" I asked.

"I know Tom does. I'm not sure about the parents. I've got enough horses for everyone, so whoever would like to go will have a horse," she concluded.

"I hate to ask but is our fearless wedding planner coming along?" I hesitated.

"I hope not! I don't think she would want to get dust all over her white leather costume. Plus I'm sure she will stay behind to oversee the barn decorations," Olivia predicted.

"I'm glad you have Carl staying behind to keep an eye on the barn. Who knows what they could get into?" I joked.

We rounded the last curve and saw that the Lincolns had already parked their car down by the corral. Shane was there with Cassandra and Grandma Laurel. I had asked Cassandra to swing by and pick him up on her way to the ranch so we could drive home together this evening.

"Where's Mama?" Olivia asked her grandmother.

"She's riding with Sarah," Laurel answered. It was cute to see the two standing side by side since they were both so tiny.

"Are you riding today?" Olivia asked her grandmother as she held her hand up to her eyes to block the bright sun.

"My riding days are long behind me, child!" Laurel giggled and hugged Olivia. "Your horses are beautiful. You take such good care of them and it shows."

"Thanks Grandma. Why don't you stay up at the farmhouse and rest this afternoon," Olivia recommended. "We're going to have a fun night tonight. I'm sure you'll be kicking up your heels 'til dawn," she joked.

"I think I could use a little rest," Laurel agreed. "That friend of yours can really shop. She drug us into so many stores, my feet are killing me!"

"Well get into the claw foot tub and soak a while. That will make you feel refreshed!" Olivia proposed.

"Here's Ruby now," I told Olivia. "Hey Sarah! Hi Ruby!"

"Hello, Amelia! Liv!" Sarah called out as she exited her

tiny Smart Car. I got a kick watching her drive it around town. I'm sure Ruby enjoyed riding with her.

"That is just the cutest car! I would love one in red," Ruby told Sarah.

"It gets great mileage." Sarah informed her. She had worn one of her themed outfits for the trail ride. A red leather vest with matching chaps, a red and white gingham shirt with mother of pearl buttons and denim jeans completed the theme.

"Wow, Sarah! You went all out," Olivia jested.

"Sarah, have you met my family?" Matt Lincoln asked politely. "This is my mother, Audrey, my father, Lewis and my brother, Tom."

"So nice to meet all of you," Sarah said casting a pleased look in Tom's direction. "I'm Sarah McCaffrey."

"Oh, yes. The tea room owner Olivia has told us so much about," Audrey spoke first. "It's so nice to meet you!"

"Will you all be joining us for the ride?" Sarah asked expectantly. Her eyes were glued on Tom's face, hoping for an affirmative answer.

"I'm allergic to horses," Audrey whined, "so I will be sitting this one out."

"Dad and I are going," Tom replied smiling at Sarah. "I hope you will be coming along."

"I wouldn't miss it for the world," she beamed at Tom while the rest of us exchanged amused glances. It was obvious Sarah was smitten by Matt's younger brother.

"Mother, why don't you wait at the ranch house? We will be starting the BBQ just as soon as we get back," Matt suggested.

"Mayday, mayday!" Olivia grabbed Cassandra's arm.

"Those two will be at it like the Hatfields and McCoys!" she whispered loudly in her friend's ear. "What am I going to do?"

"Do about what?" Cassandra asked puzzled by Olivia's remark.

"Ruby and Audrey are both going to wait at the farmhouse while we are on the trail ride. I didn't know Audrey was allergic to horses!"

"I'll handle it, don't you worry!" Cassandra reassured her best friend. "Audrey, won't you join me for a Mojito at the farmhouse? I've made a fresh batch!" Cassandra proposed to the Dallas socialite. "We can chit chat and get acquainted."

"Sounds lovely," Audrey agreed.

"I'll drive everyone up," Cassandra offered and Olivia gave her a smile that expressed her thanks.

"Mama, you behave," Olivia reminded Ruby.

"I will be the model of decorum," Ruby promised as she got in the back seat with Laurel.

"Everyone ready who's riding?" Olivia asked the group gathered at the corral. "Dan will help you mount and get your stirrups fitted."

"I'm as ready as I'll ever be," I answered. Nothing, but nothing could have prepared me for what lay ahead!

SEVEN

"That was a great ride! The views are breathtaking on top of the ridge," Sarah sighed contentedly as she swung her leg around to dismount her mare Annie.

"Here, let me give you a hand," Tom moved towards her and grabbed her around the waist. He softly eased her to the ground. She spun around and tipped her head back to admire her tall helper.

"Thank you, Tom!" she grinned with sheer delight.

"My pleasure, little lady!" he clowned and took his hat off and swept it in a low bow. "Can I escort you to the BBQ?" he said offering the crook of his arm to her.

"Why I thought you'd never ask!" Sarah said relishing the male attention from Lincoln's handsome brother.

"Amelia, are you watching this?" Shane asked amused. "Those two have been riding side-by-side the entire afternoon."

"Believe me, I've noticed. I hope she's not falling head-over-heels again," I said darkly. "Sarah wears her heart on her sleeve and gets hurt easily."

"She's a big girl. Let her have some fun," Shane advised.

"I'm not going to rain on her parade. I just would like to see her in a good relationship for a change. She deserves it!" I said as I led Max to the corral.

"Relax. Tom will be a nice escort at the wedding for Sarah. He lives in Dallas and long distance relationships fizzle out fast. She should just have fun and keep things light," he said in a fatherly manner.

"Maybe we should just mind our own business," I advised as I gave him a quick kiss. "There's been too much meddling this week from the in-laws. I think it may be contagious," I joked.

"Speaking of meddling, here is Aunt Imogene," he remarked.

"Whoo hoo, Amelia! We're here!" Imogene called out as she walked on her tip toes in the gravel. Her four inch stiletto boots were making her path to the picnic area hazardous.

"Hey Aunt Imogene! Hi Lucy! So glad you could make it for the BBQ," I said hugging my favorite aunt close to me. "You look smashing. Is this a new outfit?"

"Oh, something I got off the clearance rack at Stein Mart. I only paid forty-eight dollars for the whole outfit including the shoes. I thought it looked appropriate for tonight," she bragged as she showed off her cow inspired trench coat with matching ankle-length skirt. The combination reminded me of a walking billboard for Chik-Fil-A. I loved Imogene's laissez-faire attitude towards fashion. She wore what she wanted to, despite fashion trends and what was appropriate for her age. That was part of her unique spirit.

"If you're not careful, one of the ranch hands will think a heifer is loose and try to lasso you," Lucy Lyle joked as she joined us.

"That's the point, Lucy. I wouldn't mind being lassoed by one of Olivia's guys. They're all pretty hot. Have you seen Bill with his shirt off?" Imogene asked friskily.

"Aunt Imogene!" I said shocked. "Bill is a married man!"

"I may be over seventy, but I'm not dead," she responded. "A girl can look, can't she?"

"You're a cougar, Imogene," Shane teased her and came over to give her a kiss on the cheek.

"Speaking of hunks, where is that good-looking Lincoln?" Imogene inquired as she saw Olivia approaching us. "You haven't lost your groom have you?"

"I'm watching you," Olivia warned playfully. "He's driving up to the farmhouse to get everyone."

"I'm so happy for you both. You make a stunning couple," Imogene said clasping Olivia's hand. "I wish you much happiness. You two remind me of my third marriage to Benjamin," she said wistfully.

"Third marriage? Just how many times have you been married?" Cassandra gasped in surprise.

"Five if you don't count the three weeks I was married to Fred Larson. I found out later he was a cross-dresser and I had the marriage annulled. I was not prepared to share my wardrobe with my husband," she blabbed.

"Oh my stars! I've heard it all!" I said doubled over with laughter. "Imogene, please stop!"

"I feel like I'm roommates with Blanche Devereaux from *The Golden Girls*. She's always ready for a conquest!" Lucy complained.

"Look, I've hooked you up with some of my former boyfriends and you haven't seemed to mind," Imogene snapped at Lucy.

"And they've all had one thing on their mind," Lucy retorted. "Not one of them was interested in a nice courtship."

"You've got to remember that we're competing with the

botoxed generation. We have to work even harder to get a man," Imogene reminded her.

"I would rather be all alone than filled with chemicals and implants just to get a man," Lucy said adamantly.

"Ladies, let's head over to the picnic tables to see if we can lend a hand," I said interrupting the discourse. Gracious me, these two did get into some heated debates. I was still surprised they had decided to share a house. They were both so independent and head strong and each had lived alone for a good number of years.

Cassandra was unloading a large tub of iced beverages. She also had brought a basket carefully filled with a large lidded pitcher of her mojitos and a portable bar to mix up more of the lime flavored concoction.

"It looks like you've brought the party," I ribbed her.

"I always bring the party," she claimed. "It's what I can't possibly screw up." Cassandra was known for having the best of the best on speed dial to cater her lavish parties. She was a self-proclaimed kitchen screw up, but she was the queen of cocktail hour and always willing to bring along a frothy pitcher of libations to our gatherings.

"Speaking of parties, how did it go with the mothers?" I inquired.

"Grandma Laurel laid down for a nap and I ended up having to take a business call from overseas. I really didn't see the two mothers this afternoon. When I finished my call, Audrey had gone for a walk and I assumed Ruby was in her room," she informed me.

"At least it was peaceful," I said thankfully. "I hope the rest of the day goes as smoothly. Here, let me help with those glasses," I said and grabbed another basket from her car.

"Thanks, Amelia. Gosh, I didn't realize how close to dinner time it was. No wonder I am so hungry," Cassandra remarked as she set up her makeshift bar.

"Never fear, the BBQ has arrived!" Olivia said as she orchestrated the unloading of the large chaffing dishes from the back of her pickup. The wafting scent of beef brisket hit us and made our stomachs involuntarily growl.

"I've got the cornbread, beans and potato salad," Sarah said as she and Tom carried large covered bowls and platters over to the long serving table.

"Where's Dixie?" Cassandra said looking around. "I told her that she's got to try your BBQ Olivia. She's going to think she's died and gone to heaven!"

The mothers and Grandma Laurel arrived next driven by Matt. Everyone eagerly unloaded from his SUV with assistance from Tom and Shane.

"I can't wait to taste Tennessee BBQ," Lewis Lincoln said rubbing his hands together in anticipation. "Matt tells me I'm really getting a treat tonight. He says it rivals Texas mesquite."

"Now wait just a gosh darn minute," Tom taunted. "I'm not sure anything can top good Texas BBQ."

"Wait until you try Olivia's," his brother said proudly. "She may convert you too!" Matt said as he put his arm around his little bride.

"And wait until you try Sarah's five baked beans. She's a legend around these parts," Olivia bragged.

"I don't know about a legend, but thanks, Liv!" Sarah blushed. "I hope everyone enjoys them."

"Did you see Dixie up at the house?" Cassandra asked the Lincolns.

"I assumed she was decorating the barn," Audrey answered. "I haven't seen her since my walk this afternoon. This is quite a beautiful place you have, Olivia."

"Thank you, Audrey," Olivia said sincerely. "I have worked really hard to develop the property."

"I can see why Matt feels at home here," she said as a smile spread across her face.

"Now you understand what Dogwood Cove has to offer, besides my beautiful bride," Matt said as he put his arm around his mother, "beautiful vistas and wonderful friends."

"Oh, please stop Matt before I start blubbering," Cassandra said dabbing her eyes.

"Shall we eat, then?" Olivia suggested. "Mama, Audrey, Grandma, please go first."

"Mojito, Audrey?" Cassandra said putting a cold cocktail glass in the mother-of-the groom's hand.

"Cheers, everyone!" Audrey offered as a quick toast.

We all sat down at the picnic tables and enjoyed the setting sun and the view of the horses in the corral, contentedly nibbling on grass and flicking their tails to swat the flies. Carl, Dan and Bill also joined us with their wives and girlfriends. It was a very festive evening under the white lights that the "Dixie's Pixies" had strung earlier in the day. It was one of those rare picture perfect moments you remember the rest of your life.

Olivia had served quite a spread. There was corn on the cob with rosemary butter along with a selection of pulled pork with sweet BBQ sauce, beef brisket, grilled potatoes and the sides we had all contributed. Aunt Imogene had brought her party staple-deviled eggs which are like southern caviar to our family and Lucy had brought a hummingbird cake.

My Meyer lemon chamomile meringue pies were in the refrigerator back at the farmhouse. I would have to leave to retrieve them.

"Shane, I'm going up to the house to get the pies. I'll be back," I told him as I stood up to get in my VW convertible.

"I'll go with you. You could use an extra pair of hands," he told me.

"Tell Dixie we are saving BBQ for her," Olivia reminded me. "Tell the 'Pixies' there is plenty for everyone."

"OK," I replied as we got into the red beetle and headed up the steep driveway. The porch lights were on at the house, but the barn was unusually dark.

"I thought they might still be working on stringing lights in the barn," I remarked to Shane.

"Yeah, I thought Audrey said they were still working on the decorations. It's strange the lights are out," he commented.

"Do you think they left for the day?" I wondered.

"I thought they were all joining us for BBQ."

"Maybe they went to the hotel to change clothes. I'd like to see what they got done in the barn today. Let's take a look!" I said grabbing his hand and walking towards the darkened barn entrance. I could hear the whinny of a horse as we approached the doorway.

"The light switch is on your right," I reminded Shane and he flipped the large switch.

"This looks great!" Shane said as the barn was flooded with what seemed like a million white lights wrapped around each rafter and beam.

"I like what they did with the curly willow arching around the doorways wrapped in the smaller twinkle lights.

It really gives it an elegant touch. And the pumpkin topiaries sitting in the urns are so whimsical. I love it!"

Dixie had done an outstanding job. Though the wedding was just two days away, the barn was really coming together. The "Pixies" would finish decorating the barn early Saturday morning after the horses had been moved out for the reception and the barn cleaned from top to bottom.

"Hey Apple Jack," I said noticing the horse hanging his head outside his stall door. "You're probably lonesome in here all by yourself, huh boy?" I asked giving him a gentle pat on his head. The horse reared back and kicked the stall door with his front hooves.

"Whoa boy, what's got you all spooked?" Shane asked approaching the stall. "Amelia, step back. He's not acting right," Shane commanded.

"He's blind in one eye," I reminded him. "All the lights are probably throwing him off," I said defending the large horse.

"Hey, big fella! It's OK," Shane said soothingly to Apple Jack. "That's it, good boy," he said petting the horse.

"Are those feed bags in the back corner of Jack's stall?" I asked pointing to what looked like white bags of grain taking up a large portion of the stall floor.

"I don't know. You hold Jack's bridle. I'm going to check it out," Shane said slowly opening the barn door and walking carefully around the horse.

"There, there, Jack," I said as I tried to keep the horse distracted. He swung his body to the side to stand as far away from Shane as he could. "What is it, Shane?"

"It's not what. It's who. It's Dixie," Shane said excitedly. "Amelia, she's dead!"

EIGHT

The barn was buzzing with activity. Crime scene investigators as well as the county coroner were busy photographing the stall. Apple Jack had long since been removed and placed across the barn as far away from the chaos as possible. Olivia, Dan, Carl and Bill were staying busy feeding the horses for the evening and doing the routine end of day chores. Olivia was stoic and unusually quiet, something that concerned all of us.

Matt was making himself useful by speaking with the detectives investigating the scene. Though he was not officially working, just his mere presence made all of us feel more comfortable.

"It looks as though Jack trampled her. There was quite a bit of blood in the stall and the horse was very agitated," Shane reported to the large group gathered on the farmhouse porch. We were all staying warm thanks to the outdoor fireplace that Olivia kept stocked with a ready supply of wood. Tom kept stoking the fire as we all listened intently.

"I heard Olivia warn Dixie and her workers to stay away from Jack. Why would she have ignored the warning and gone into his stall anyway? I can't believe she is dead!" Cassandra sniffed as big tears streamed down her face. "Dixie and I have quite a history. She has helped me through the years with baby showers, bridal parties, Doug's campaign fund raising events and now she's gone! I still can't believe it!" she sobbed as her body shook in the cold night.

"Here baby, drink this," Ruby soothed Cassandra's hair and handed her a hot mug of coffee. "I think you need a blanket. You're shivering out here," she said with a worried expression on her face. "Maybe you should go inside."

"No, I want to know what happened to her. And where is her crew? I called Austin's cell phone and no one is answering. Someone has got to tell them what happened to Dixie," Cassandra insisted. "They need to know. Arrangements will have to be made and her family will need to be notified."

"Here, Cassandra. Wrap up in this if you are going to stay out here," Sarah said covering her shoulders with a quilt. "We all want to know what happened to Dixie and we will help in any way we can." She patted her friend on the back and sat down next to her.

"What in the world made her go into that stall?" Audrey thought aloud. "I certainly wouldn't think of venturing into an unknown horse's stall unless I really was comfortable handling horses. In my opinion, that's asking for trouble."

"She certainly was taking a chance," Lewis agreed. "Whatever she was doing, she should have waited for Olivia to handle that wild horse."

"Jack is *not* wild! Why must everyone assume it was the horse's fault?" Olivia said defensively as she walked onto the porch. "He is one of my best horses. He's very protective of his right side since he lost his eye two years ago."

"Olivia, of course Jack didn't *try* to hurt Dixie," Audrey predicted. "He was just doing what a wild animal would do. It was an accident."

"Audrey, Jack is not some wild animal! He is one of my prized quarter horses. I broke that horse myself. I've had some of my most challenged kids ride him and he has always been gentle. Jack would never hurt anyone, *period!*"

"Calm down, Liv. No one is trying to say it was his fault," I reassured her. "He was acting pretty riled up this afternoon. Its possible Dixie spooked him and he reared up. That would be a normal reaction," I concluded.

"How could this have happened?" Olivia started crying. "I tried to tell everyone to leave Jack alone. What was she thinking going into his stall? And now she's dead! All these years, I've run Riverbend Ranch under close supervision. We've never had an accident! I can't believe this happened. I knew not to go on that trail ride and leave those people unattended in the barn. This could have been prevented!" She stormed into the house. A loud slam of the screen door made everyone jump. Olivia was more than agitated. She was livid.

"I'll go after her," Grandmother Laurel said as she rose from her rocking chair. "She shouldn't blame herself for what happened."

"Oh dear," Sarah moaned. "And two days before the wedding."

"Olivia's wedding!" Cassandra cried leaning on Shane. "This has ruined everything!"

"Let's just take this one hour at a time," Shane said reassuring a hysterical Cassandra. "The police will do their job and we will worry about the wedding later."

He looked at me across the porch with raised eyebrows. He didn't know any more than I did what would become of the wedding plans. Right now, we had to notify Dixie's family and move forward with helping them make arrangements. Where could Austin be and why wasn't he returning Cassandra's phone calls?

Tom stoked the fire a bit more and stared into the embers. He looked lost in thought as we all quietly sat around, feeling totally helpless.

"I should call Doug," Cassandra thought aloud. "He will want to issue some sort of statement. Dixie was part of his team when he ran for the house of representatives. She saw to every detail from lighting him properly during his campaign speeches, to organizing his fundraising dinners, to decorating for his inaugural party. He will most certainly want to be notified. This will crush him."

"Is he in Nashville tonight?" I asked.

"He should be almost home by now. He is driving in this weekend for the wedding. He wouldn't miss giving Olivia away," she said deep in thought. She rose from her seat leaving the quilt behind and walked a distance from the house, I assumed to have some privacy when she called Doug.

"Aunt Imogene, Lucy, you two should go home. It's getting late and the temperature is dropping. Why don't I call you tomorrow morning with updates," I suggested worrying about them both getting ill from the chill. A fog had rolled in and covered the hillside with a dense layer. The ranch lights cast an eerie glow around the property. The air was heavy and moist and I felt myself involuntarily shiver.

"I don't mind staying. My Twitter followers and Facebook friends are going to want updates. No one can believe this happened to poor Dixie!" she confessed.

"You've been Tweeting this?" I asked incredulously.

"I'm personally devastated," Imogene claimed. "I can't believe this freak accident happened right here on Olivia's ranch!"

"Where's Olivia?" Dan asked as he strode onto the porch. "I need her right now," he said urgently. "The police have called animal control to haul Jack away. They consider him too dangerous to leave at the ranch!" he said angrily shaking his head. "I know that horse and he's no killer!" the ranch hand said tipping his head back and wiping his face with both of his hands.

"I'll go get her," Sarah offered nervously.

"What do they want with Jack?" Ruby asked concerned.

"They're talking about putting him down," Dan told us. "That would kill Olivia," he remarked.

"Over my dead body," Olivia said through gritted teeth as she pushed open the screen door. "No one is loading up Jack, you hear me Dan? No one!" she yelled and headed towards the barn with her fists clenched and a determined look on her face.

"It's a good thing Matt is down there," Shane pronounced. "There's going to be trouble if they try to touch that horse."

"Maybe they need to do some forensic observations like photograph blood spatters on Jack's coat or take molds of his hooves," Sarah deducted.

"You sound like you have been involved in an investigation before. You seem very knowledgeable about this," Audrey noted.

"I read a lot and watch CSI," she sheepishly admitted. "I would think they need to take Jack in order to gather evidence."

"We better get down there and calm Olivia down," I thought aloud. "She is so passionate about her horses. Who knows what she will do?" I started walking down the gravel driveway to the barn. I could hear yelling as I got closer to the large red structure.

"I will not let you do this to Jack! He's not a killer and you don't have my permission to take him!" she could be heard screaming loudly from within.

"Calm down, Liv. They're just doing their job," Lincoln spoke up loudly.

I walked through the doorway and was shocked to see Matt Lincoln holding back his fiancée while the sheriff faced them.

"You leave me no choice but to impound the animal and take you into custody for interfering with an official investigation," the officer shouted. "Is this really what you want? Why not cooperate and let us take the animal?"

"Because you want to put him down," she cried. "He would no more hurt you than he would a child. I raised Jack myself since he was three months old. He wouldn't do this. I am refusing to let you take him." She crossed her arms and tilted her head back, looking up at the sheriff with defiance. "Do what you will with me, but don't touch Jack."

"Liv, please honey, cooperate. I will personally see to it that Jack is unharmed," Lincoln begged her.

"I'm sorry, Matt, but I can't trust that you can stop them. It is entirely my fault that Jack is in this situation. I shouldn't have left the barn. This would not have happened," she told him.

"Turn around and put your hands behind your back," the officer ordered her.

"Nelson, is this really necessary?" Lincoln barked.

"Sorry, Matt, but she's breaking the law. You have the right to remain silent," he said snapping his cuffs around Olivia's tiny wrists. "Anything you say can and shall be used against you. You have the right to an attorney," he continued.

"Hold it right there, mister!" Ruby Rivers shrieked as she ran towards her daughter. You're not taking her anywhere!" she yelled shaking her finger in the officer's face.

"Step back ma'am or I will charge you with obstruction of justice!" he warned. "Duke, get another officer over here. I need backup," he radioed his colleagues.

"Stop it, Mama! Get back!" Olivia ordered.

"What the hell is going on here, Matt?" Lewis Lincoln bellowed. "Can't you get this under control?"

"Did you hear what I said? Uncuff my daughter now!" Ruby demanded as she pounded her fists into the officer's chest.

"Matt, talk some sense into her," Olivia advised her groom, "or she is going to end up sharing a jail cell with me."

A group of three officers rushed over to where Ruby stood.

"Take her into custody. She assaulted an officer," Nelson informed the trio.

"What? You've got to be kidding!" Ruby exclaimed. "If I were going to assault an officer, I would do something more like this," she said kicking sawdust with her boot directly into Officer Nelson's face.

"Cuff her," he ordered as he stepped back wiping his eyes. A cloud of saw dust filled the air and we all began coughing.

"Come on Nelson, tensions are high. She's harmless," Lincoln claimed. "She's Olivia's mother for goodness sake!"

"Not my problem, Lincoln. I'd say you have your hands full with these two red heads," Nelson concluded shaking his head back and forth. "I've got to book her. She left me no choice."

Aunt Imogene was recording the whole scene on her phone. We all stood around with our mouths hanging open, not knowing what we should or could say at this point to diffuse the scene around us.

"Don't worry, Mama! I'll have Cassandra send her attorney. He'll get us out of this mess!"

"Don't worry about me, baby girl. I'll be fine. You take care of you right now," she said defiantly as the officers led her to the squad car.

"What in the world is going on here?" Cassandra asked as she walked into the barn. It did seem like mass hysteria had broken out around us. "Why is Ruby being led away to a squad car handcuffed? And why is Olivia in cuffs, Lincoln?"

"Not now, Cassandra!" Lincoln snapped.

"Ruby assaulted an officer by kicking sawdust in his face," I quietly informed her. "She was upset that he had cuffed Olivia."

"I'm upset they've cuffed Olivia. And for what, may I ask? I'm calling my attorney Thomas Simpson right now!" she threatened the officer.

"You can tell Mr. Simpson that she is being charged with obstruction and her sweet mother is being charged with assault of an officer," he said wiping his face with the back of his arm.

"Don't worry, Liv. Thomas will have you out of this jam in no time," Cassandra said authoritatively. "My husband is Congressman Doug Reynolds. I will personally see that he looks into this himself. Heads are going to roll if this has been handled inappropriately. This seems more like martial law than an investigation."

"Don't worry, Cassandra. I've got it all recorded," Imogene piped up.

Officer Nelson began to look about nervously. "Threaten me all you want to ladies, but I'm just doing my job. Now if you don't mind, I'm taking Ms. Rivers into custody."

"Hold on, Nelson. Don't take her anywhere. It wasn't the horse." A detective, emerging from the crime scene joined us. "This was definitely a murder staged to look like an accident. We've got the evidence to prove it!"

NINE

"Murder? Are you sure? Why murder Dixie?" Cassandra asked aloud. "I can't believe it. This is getting worse by the minute!"

"You knew the vic well?" the detective questioned Cassandra.

"And you are?" she asked pulling herself up straight and wiping her eyes.

"Dave Mansfield," Lincoln said as a means of introduction. "This is Cassandra Reynolds. She has known Dixie for years. The deceased was our wedding planner," he informed the overweight officer.

"Tough break. I'm Sorry. Lincoln, looks like this is a crime scene. I'm going to need to question everybody, so please, take everyone up to the house. Mrs. Reynolds, I would like to begin with you," Mansfield said solemnly.

"What makes you think this is a homicide?" Lincoln questioned his co-worker.

"We found blood droplets in front of the stall door in the hallway. The contusion on her head is consistent with blunt force trauma. The scuff marks on her boot heels indicate she was dragged into the stall. She was dead before she was taken into that stall and I'm willing to bet the evidence will back it up. She was definitely hit from behind and this was staged to look like an accident," Detective Mansfield stated.

"Wait. What about my mother?" Olivia asked still cuffed. "She didn't know what she was doing. She was angry."

"I'm sorry Ms. Rivers, but we're taking your mother down to the precinct. She is being charged with assaulting an officer," Officer Nelson informed her. "We're still going to need to take your horse to our lab. I promise you can come along with him and stay with him as long as you wish. We just need to take some photographs and process any forensics we find."

"That horse was in the stall with the killer. He may have some trace evidence on him that will help us find who did this," Detective Mansfield concurred.

"So no more talk of killer animal, then? You're not going to put Jack down?" Olivia said calming herself.

"No, ma'am," the police officer said unlocking her cuffs. She rubbed her wrists together and threw her arms around Lincoln.

"I'm going with Jack," she informed him. "You help Mama, OK?" she said and lifted up on her toes to kiss him.

"I'll head to the station. I'll see if I can get the charges against her reduced," Lincoln told her. "I promise, Liv. We'll get to the bottom of this!" he said and headed towards his car. He nodded to his parents and brother as he passed them.

"Detective Mansfield, please make yourself at home. My foreman Dan will help you with anything you need on the property. I'm going to get Jack ready," she told him and headed to the horse's stall.

"What in the world is going on?" a dazed Audrey Lincoln asked her husband as she watched her son's tail lights disappear down the long driveway.

"I'm not sure. I think we are all going to be questioned about Dixie," he told his wife.

"I don't know what they think they are going to gain by questioning us. We were all at the BBQ when Dixie and her crew were at the barn. It could have been any number of people," she observed.

Yes, Audrey, it could have been any number of people. But mingling amongst us was a killer, someone who was clever enough to stage a murder to look like an accident and dangerous enough to kill again.

TEN

"*D*id you get in touch with Doug? Is he on his way over?" Shane asked a shaky Cassandra.

We were all inside gathered around the arched brick fireplace trying to warm up. Our group filled the large comfortable kitchen as we took seats around the ten foot long antique trestle table. I made pots of hot tea as Sarah continued rummaging around the pantry looking for ideas of what to prepare for a snack. It was going to be a long night and we would all need caffeine and sustenance to get through this nightmare.

"I didn't reach him. His phone went straight to voicemail. I left a message. He may already be home. I should try the house phone," a distracted Cassandra thought aloud. She stood next to the large window and watched the thick fog rolling across the Tennessee River.

"Why don't I try to reach him for you," Shane suggested gently leading her back to the table. "You just sit over here and get warm next to the fire. I know this has got to be hard on you Cassandra."

"Who in the world would want to hurt Dixie? She was a well-respected fixture in the Hollywood and Washington DC communities. What would anyone possibly gain by killing her?" she lamented.

"Precisely," Detective Mansfield concurred as he walked into the homey kitchen. "I need your help Mrs. Reynolds to compile a list of everyone you can remember that came into contact with the victim since she's been in town. I've been told she was from Hollywood and was hired to oversee the wedding this weekend."

"Yes. I have known and worked with Dixie for years. I still can't believe this!" Cassandra said breaking down. She began sobbing inconsolably and put her head down on the table.

"Detective, I don't think she's in any condition to be questioned right now. Maybe we should get in touch with her husband and let her rest for a bit. She was very close with Ms. Beauregard and is really taking this hard," I suggested.

"I'm fine, Amelia. Really, I am. I will be more than happy to help you, detective," she said trying to compose herself.

"Shane, did you get Doug on the phone? He needs to get over here right away," I said taking him aside.

"I couldn't reach him. He didn't answer his cell phone or the house phone. I'm not sure where he is," he confided quietly.

"This is becoming a regular pattern with our good friend, Doug. He never seems to be around when Cassandra needs him the most. When you do get a hold of him, I'm going to give him a piece of my mind!" I threatened. I was not one to interfere, but my close friend was floundering and needed the support of her husband.

"I think it's probably best to stay out of it," he opined. "We don't need to go meddling into other couple's lives."

"Are you forgetting how unsupportive he was of Cassandra in Savannah? His wife was being questioned by the police and he didn't even bother to interrupt his campaigning to be with her. He sent Thomas Simpson in his place," I fumed.

"Hush, Amelia. Keep your voice down. We don't want to upset her any further." He pulled me outside to the porch and we continued to talk in low whispers. "I know what happened. I was just hoping that he was a little less self-centered now that the campaign has been over for six months."

"Don't count on it, Shane. I think Doug is narcissistic and when there's smoke, there's usually a fire!"

"What are you talking about?" Shane asked. "What smoke?"

"The smoke I'm referring to is multiple rumors about Doug and his young campaign manager, Penelope. You've heard the gossip around town. And don't tell me you didn't notice her at the inaugural ball! She was practically hanging all over Doug. It was quite a display."

"The lady in the red dress with the cut outs in strategic areas? No, I can't say I remember her," Shane teased.

"It's not funny, Shane. Cassandra's marriage is in trouble. I'm worried about her. Doug doesn't spend time with her. He is never home, living most of the time halfway across the state in Nashville. Meanwhile, she's in Dogwood Cove running his *family's* business. It's not a good situation at all!"

"We've been friends with Doug and Cassandra for years. I would rather not take sides, but I will say that he has not been himself since he started running for office. I'll keep trying his numbers until I get a hold of him. I'm sure there's a good explanation as to why he's not answering."

"I'm going back inside and see if I can help Cassandra come up with the contact list Detective Mansfield requested. Did you speak to Aunt Alice?"

"I called her about twenty minutes ago. She says the kids are in bed and she will just make herself at home in the guest room. She was very upset to hear about Dixie. She told me she's available to stay the rest of the weekend."

"She is such a lifesaver! How thoughtful of her. I don't want Emma and Charlie to hear about this. They don't need to start worrying about a murderer on the loose in Dogwood Cove," I said expressing concern over our children.

Shane's Aunt Alice had always offered to help when we were in need of an extra pair of hands with the kids and when we owned the tea room. She had run a restaurant herself and was a one-woman wonder in my book. Just knowing she was with the children helped me to relax and focus my attention back on the investigation.

Shane took out his cell phone to call Doug and I headed back inside. At least it was warm inside the welcoming kitchen. Detective Mansfield was speaking with Audrey and asking some very pointed questions.

"So you did not actually know the victim?" he asked scribbling notes in a small binder.

"No. We're from Dallas and in town for our son's wedding. I met Ms. Beauregard for the first time earlier today when we gathered here for the trail ride," she said folding her hands together.

"So you were on the trail ride with the rest of the wedding party?"

"No, I was not. I'm allergic to horses, so I opted to come up to the farmhouse and visit with Mrs. Reynolds while everyone else went on the ride," she informed him.

"And you were with Mrs. Reynolds at the farmhouse the entire time?"

"Well, not the entire time. Cassandra had to take a business call and she excused herself. I waited a while and then decided to take a walk," she continued.

"Were you with anyone when you went for the walk?"

"No. Ruby was taking a bubble bath and Laurel was taking a nap. So I went by myself," she calmly said.

"Where did you go when you took this walk?" he said looking straight into Audrey's eyes. Her husband looked around from the fireplace, concern apparent on his face.

"I went down by the river and walked the perimeter of the property." She took a sip of her tea and placed her tea cup down.

"How long were you gone? Thank you," he said to Sarah as he accepted a mug of steaming coffee.

"I'm not sure. I didn't check the time. I guess I was gone for about an hour or so."

"And no one saw you during your walk? Maybe one of the ranch hands?" he continued questioning her. I had seen that look before and Audrey's alibi was sounding very weak at best.

"No. Everyone had gone on the trail ride including the ranch hands. The only people left were Dixie and her team who were decorating the barn and those of us at the farmhouse. It was rather quiet and peaceful," she elaborated.

"Were you near the barn at any time?" he pushed.

"Audrey, don't say another word," her husband stopped her.

"Why, Lewis? I have nothing to hide. Yes, I did go up to the barn. That was at the end of my walk when I was heading back to the farmhouse. No one was in the barn when I arrived."

"Did you see anyone suspicious or hear anything? A scuffle? An argument?"

"No, it was very quiet which I thought was odd since Dixie was supposed to be decorating the barn for the wedding. And like I said earlier, I'm allergic to horses, so I didn't spend much time in the barn. I was looking around to see the progress for the wedding. I stayed maybe five minutes at the most."

"And then what happened?" Detective Mansfield asked relentlessly.

"I went back to the farmhouse and met up with Cassandra. Laurel was up from her nap and Ruby was finished getting ready for the BBQ. We all rode together to the BBQ. That's about it," she said nonchalantly.

"So Mrs. Reynolds was here at the farmhouse when you got back, correct?"

"Yes, I was. I had finished my overseas call and was here in the kitchen when Audrey came back from her walk," Cassandra spoke up.

"And what time was that?" Detective Mansfield asked turning his attention to Cassandra.

"Well, I can check my phone log to see what time I received the call from my Paris office and how long I was on the phone. I would say it was close to five PM." She offered.

"Yes, I'm going to need to see your phone records to verify Mrs. Lincoln's timeline."

"Yes, please verify all you need to, detective," Audrey volunteered.

"Does anyone know where the victim and her employees were staying or how I can get a hold of them?" he queried.

"They were staying at the Dogwood Inn on Main Street. I have Austin's phone number, but he hasn't been answering. I've tried to call him several times with no luck," Cassandra explained.

"I'll send an officer over there to see what's going on. It could be that everyone is sleeping at this late hour," he surmised.

"They were invited to the BBQ following the trail ride," I told him. "They helped hang the lights around the picnic area and were supposed to join us for the food and bonfire after they finished decorating the barn."

"And no one showed up? Did you see them leave the property?" he turned and asked me as I stood at the sink washing dishes and trying to stay busy. Anything to keep my mind occupied.

"I didn't see anyone leave the property after we got back from the trail ride. The main gate is just past the corral where we had the horses. Anyone leaving would have had to come by us," Shane spoke up.

"So, it's safe to assume they left at some point before you were back from the trail ride," he thought aloud. "It would have been before five PM if Mrs. Reynolds timeline is correct. Interesting. And Mrs. Lincoln, you didn't see them leaving the property while you were on your walk?"

"No, but they could have left while I was down by the river. I did think it was rather odd that no one was around the barn when I went inside."

"I thought it strange that Dixie didn't come for the BBQ, but I assumed that she was busy overseeing all the decorating details at the barn. That wouldn't be unusual for her since she was a micromanager," Cassandra remarked.

"Have you put together a list of who Ms. Beauregard encountered while she was here in Dogwood Cove?"

"Yes, I've got a partial list. There were a lot of people Dixie met with including florists, caterers, bluegrass bands, equipment vendors, ice sculptors, limousine services. It's pretty extensive, but I should be able to work on it and get it to you in the morning," she suggested.

"That would be great. Now Mrs. Rivers, you were at the farmhouse during the trail ride, correct?" he said turning his attention to a very tired and quiet Laurel Rivers who was sitting in a corner armchair near the fireplace.

"Yes, I was here with Ruby, Cassandra and Audrey. I don't ride much anymore at my age," she smiled gently at the officer.

"I realize your daughter isn't here right now for me to ask, but we can always question her at the station. Were you here with her the entire time?"

"I lay down in the guest room to take a nap. I was tuckered out from shopping earlier in the day," she explained looking sweetly at Cassandra.

"And where was your daughter while you were taking a nap? Here in the farm house?" he continued.

"She was in the master bathroom taking a bubble bath. Olivia had suggested we soak our feet after our marathon shopping today," she replied.

"And you took a nap while she was taking a bath, is that right?" he repeated.

"Yes."

"And how long were you asleep?" he persisted.

"Maybe a half an hour," she stated calmly.

"Did you look at a clock or a watch?"

"No I did not," she responded.

"So you are not actually sure how long you were asleep, correct?"

"I guess not. What are you trying to say, detective?"

"It's obvious that neither you nor your daughter Ruby have an alibi during the trail ride," he countered.

"How can you assume that?" Sarah inquired placing a tray of sandwiches on the long trestle table.

"Mrs. Reynolds was taking an overseas call, Mrs. Lincoln was out on a walk, and Mrs. Rivers was taking a nap. No one was actually with Ruby. Maybe she was not in the bathroom at all. Maybe she never took a bath. Maybe Laurel Rivers never took a nap. Who knows?"

"That's preposterous!" Audrey Lincoln shouted. "Laurel and Ruby are about as guilty as I am."

"That's what I'm getting at. None of you had an alibi. Any one of you could have gone to the barn and killed Dixie Beauregard. Which one of you had the motive? That's what I'm going to find out."

"You're barking up the wrong tree, detective!" Sarah said grabbing his plate away from him. She didn't like his accusations and didn't find him deserving of her sandwich.

"There is no way Ruby, Grandmother Laurel or Audrey had anything to do with Dixie's murder. I can vouch for all of them," I declared coming around the table to face the overweight detective.

"I would have to disagree with you, Ma'am. From the display I saw tonight towards Officer Nelson, I think it's safe to say that Mrs. Rivers has quite an explosive temper. People like that can become unhinged and do all sorts of unspeakable things when provoked," he retorted.

"Ruby may be fiery, but she had no cause to hurt Dixie," I lectured him. "She hardly knew the woman."

"Detective, I think you are on a wild goose chase," Cassandra argued. "None of these ladies had a reason to kill Dixie. I think the best way to proceed is to question her employees. Why did they leave so early? Why didn't they attend the BBQ? Someone saw something or knows something. I would start with them."

"Get that list together for me and it goes without saying, none of you needs to leave town in case I have some more questions," he concluded.

"We understand, detective," Shane said speaking up. "If we can be of any further assistance, please contact us."

"I will be in touch with all of you. I'm sorry for your loss, Mrs. Reynolds. Try to get some rest and I will speak with you in the morning about your contact list and phone log."

"Absolutely Detective. Thank you," Cassandra said shaking her head. We watched as he exited through the screen door and headed back towards the barn.

"I think we all need to get some sleep. Cassandra, I think I should give you a ride home. You're not in any condition to drive," Shane recommended.

"I think I will take you up on that, Shane if it's not too much trouble."

"Grandmother Laurel. Would you like some company tonight?" Sarah proposed. "I don't think you need to be here by yourself with all the police activity around the barn. Why don't I stay with you and help with the farm activities in the morning."

"That would be nice honey. I'm not sure I can sleep tonight knowing Ruby is locked up and Olivia's wedding is ruined. Not to mention there's a murderer on the loose!"

I had forgotten about the murderer being on the loose. Laurel was right. I was so focused on proving it wasn't Ruby or Audrey that I had almost forgotten a killer was walking the streets of our sleepy mountain community.

"Would you feel better having a man around to protect you?" Tom proposed. "I'd be happy to stay."

"I would feel better, that is if you would Grandmother Laurel," Sarah said beaming towards the tall ruggedly handsome Texan.

"I think that would be a good idea under the circumstances," Lewis Lincoln agreed. "Audrey and I will head to the General Morgan Inn and be back first thing in the morning. We've got to put our heads together to figure out what to do about this wedding."

"I would assume the wedding would be cancelled with a murder investigation going on," Audrey implied as she shot a perturbed look at her husband.

"Dixie would want Olivia to go ahead with the wedding. She was a perfectionist. She thought of her clients first. She would not want Olivia's special day ruined," Cassandra presumed. "We need to get in touch with her team and see what we can salvage for the wedding."

"We can talk about all this tomorrow. Let's get some rest and reconvene in the morning. Our first task will be to get Ruby out of jail," I reminded the group.

"Thomas is going over to the courthouse in the morning for her arraignment," Cassandra informed us. "She has to appear before the judge at nine AM."

"Then, I will need a ride to the courthouse," Laurel spoke up.

"Consider it done. I'll pick you up at eight-thirty. That should be plenty of time for us to get there," Shane said.

"I will get my list to the detective in the morning. Am I forgetting anything?"

ELEVEN

"*Where's* Austin?" Cassandra asked the ponytailed "pixie" eating breakfast in the dining room of the Dogwood Inn. Her co-workers were present and busily consuming their morning meals dressed in their mandatory all black garb. None of them looked very concerned or upset. I assumed they didn't know about Dixie's demise.

"I haven't seen Austin since we were at the ranch yesterday. Have you seen him Sam?" she turned and asked the woman with black spiked hair sitting at the next table.

"Haven't seen him? Do you need him for something?" she responded as she took another bite of bagel and cream cheese.

"I think all of you need to know that Dixie was found murdered last night," Cassandra informed the group. Audible gasps could be heard in the dining room. It was an apparent surprise for them.

"What? No! Dixie murdered?" Miss ponytail said shocked. "What happened?"

"She was hit from behind and dragged into one of the stalls in the barn. My husband and I found her last night," I informed her.

"Say what? I thought something was wrong when she wasn't here at eight AM sharp for our morning meeting," a redheaded "pixie" spoke up.

"Who would want to hurt Dixie? Any ideas?" Cassandra inquired.

A hush fell over the room as Dixie's employees began looking around uneasily at each other as if none of them wanted to be the first to speak.

"Look, I know this has come as a real shock to you, but we've got to figure out who killed her. The police are going to come asking questions, so you might as well start spilling the beans," Cassandra warned them.

"Dixie wasn't the easiest person to get along with. She could really tick people off," one lanky brunette male offered up. "She had a lot of competition in her line of business. Any one of her competitors would be glad to see her gone."

"Marcus is right," the ponytail agreed. "She had the lion's share of the celebrity wedding market cornered and there are a lot of event planners in Hollywood who will be happy with news."

"I can't imagine being happy to hear that a competitor has been murdered," Cassandra remarked. "How incredibly twisted is that?"

"Hollywood is a cut-throat town. Don't forget that!" Marcus warned.

We both pulled up chairs as we tried to question and console the group at the same time, though there were not many tears shed. Strangely, they seemed more in shock than upset.

"So where is Austin? He's Dixie's righthand from what I gathered working with her in the past," Cassandra continued.

There was another pregnant pause as the assemblage looked at each other.

"What? What aren't you telling me? Out with it. You guys have worked with me many times. You can trust me," Cassandra pleaded.

"Austin isn't just Dixie's right hand man, he's her secret lover," Marcus confessed.

"You've got to be kidding me?" I said shocked. "He looks to be only twenty-five and Dixie was much older."

"Actually he is twenty-three and cougars are pretty notorious in Hollywood. Dixie was no exception," Sam told us. She had applied so much hair product, I wondered if she could use her spikes as a weapon.

"And was it common knowledge? Was she very open with her relationship?" I asked.

"No, absolutely not. Dixie was extremely private. We knew because when you spend a lot of hours with co-workers, you pick up on things," the ponytail surmised.

"She never mentioned it to me," Cassandra said.

"She would never have told you," another male clad in black added. "She was a consummate professional."

"Are you sure? I still can't picture Dixie and Austin," I said astonished.

"Believe it, sister! Dixie and Austin went on trips together, especially Las Vegas. She was a great event planner, but Dixie had her demons," Marcus said emphatically crossing his arms and shaking his head up and down.

"Demons? Dixie? What kind of demons?" Cassandra asked sounding alarmed.

"Well the need to look young. She was constantly having a nip here, a tuck there," Sam demonstrated pulling the skin tight on the sides of her face. "She was a plastic surgeon's dream!"

"Joan Rivers had nothing on Dixie," the red head added. "She took off a whole month last winter during the slow season to recover from having a total facelift including cheek implants, a tummy tuck and liposuction. She was in a terrible amount of pain!"

"How do you know all this? I thought we were close and I had no idea. I just thought she took great care of herself," Cassandra questioned the young lady closely.

"Because I took care of her. I got her mail, walked Trixie, prepared meals, took her to the doctor, anything she needed to have done while she was away 'on a three week cruise' is what she had me tell everyone," she concluded.

"Why all the secrecy about plastic surgery? People are pretty open about that these days, or so I thought they were," I speculated.

"Dixie didn't want anyone to know her age. When you work in Hollywood, the young and beautiful people get all the jobs. She had mega competition from party planners much younger than herself and she told me on more than one occasion that people hired her based on her appearance. She felt extreme pressure to keep up with the younger up and coming event planners. It's brutal in California!" Marcus informed us.

"Marcus, you said demons, as in plural. What else do you know about?" I piped up.

"I think you better talk to Austin about that. I don't want to gossip about other people's business," he said.

Funny, they all seemed just fine discussing the plastic surgery. I didn't think helping to find Dixie's killer was gossiping. There was more to this event planner than what was on the surface. Dixie had as many layers as an onion from what I was hearing from a need to look young to the need to feel young by dating much younger men.

"So where is he?" I said point blank. "We need to talk to him and so do the police."

"I haven't seen him since we finished decorating the barn," Sam admitted.

"What happened at the barn? Did anyone see anything, hear anything?" Cassandra asked intently.

"Yeah, you were all supposed to come to the BBQ and the bonfire. Why did you leave so early?" I jumped in.

"We were asked to," the ponytail informed us. "Dixie said we could go back to the inn, freshen up and then we would meet in the reception area to come back to the ranch around six o'clock. She never met us."

"Did you not think that was odd? Did you try to call her?" Cassandra grilled the young girl.

"Odd, no. It's happened before. Especially when she and Austin are fighting," she claimed.

"There was a fight between Dixie and Austin? When?" I asked intently.

"Georgia, you shouldn't have said anything. You'll get that poor guy in trouble," Marcus chastised her.

"The police are going to find out anyway. I'm just being honest," Georgia turned and defended herself. "Austin and Dixie had a fight in the barn. Dixie sent us back to the inn so she could talk with him privately."

"What were they fighting about?" I pushed. I was not about to let up on this young lady while she was in a talkative mood. I shot a daggered look at Marcus to keep quiet.

"Dixie was in the hayloft with one of the ranch guys. Austin caught them together and all hell broke loose!" she continued.

"A ranch guy? Are you sure?" I said in total disbelief. Olivia was very particular about whom she hired to work on the ranch. Most of the ranch hands had been with her for ten plus years. I was having a hard time picturing any of them with Dixie. That didn't fit with the loyal, driven, polite men that I personally knew at Riverbend Ranch. Something wasn't adding up.

"Thanks for the information. I think we know where to check next," Cassandra said grabbing her handbag to go. "If any of you hear from Austin, please contact me immediately," she requested. "You have my cell phone number."

"We sure will, Mrs. Reynolds," Marcus reassured her. "If we can do anything for you, will you let us know?"

"Actually, there *is* something you can help me with…"

TWELVE

"There's one more thing I want to do before we go," Cassandra said leading the way to the antique front desk. "Margaret, what room is Austin staying in?" she questioned the pleasant innkeeper.

"The cute blonde Brad Pitt look-a-like?" Margaret Dunn said as her face lit up. "He's on the third floor in room 312 right up the front stairs."

"Thanks, Margaret. Have a good day," Cassandra said pulling her handbag over her shoulder, a determined look evident on her face. "We'll just pay Mr. Austin a call and ask him what happened at the barn yesterday afternoon. I'm determined to get to the bottom of this," she informed me.

"Hold on a minute. I'm getting a call from Shane," I stopped at the bottom of the grand curving stair case that looked like something straight out of the movie set from *Gone with the Wind*. "Any news, Shane?"

"Ruby just finished her hearing before the judge and the DA charged her with disorderly conduct instead of assault of an officer. They decided to drop the charges because this is her first offense," he happily told me.

"Oh, thank goodness!" I exclaimed and gave Cassandra the thumbs up. "So you are headed back to the ranch?"

"Not quite yet. We have to check out her belongings at the holding locker and then we will be heading back."

"That shouldn't take too long. Is Olivia there with you?" I asked breathlessly as we began climbing the massive staircase.

"She's still with Jack, but she was elated to hear about Ruby. You sound winded. What are you doing?" he asked.

"Cassandra and I are at the Dogwood Inn talking with Dixie's people. Austin was noticeably absent, so we are on our way to his room right now. It's on the third floor. I think I better get back into my yoga class as soon as the wedding is over. I am out of shape!" I admitted.

"I'll call you just as soon as I take Ruby and Laurel back to the ranch," he promised as our phone call came to a close.

"His room should be just down the hall to the right," Cassandra said as we turned at the top of the staircase. The hallway was lined with original paintings by our local artists depicting historic buildings in Dogwood Cove. It was a charming inn and Margaret had done an excellent job of preserving the magnificent home built by the town's founding father in the 1870's.

"Here it is," I said as we read "Room 312" on the brass plaque. I knocked softly and waited for the door to open.

"You're going to have to knock louder than that, Amelia," Cassandra said rapping loudly on the solid mahogany door. We waited impatiently as we stared at the door.

"I haven't seen him since yesterday morning," Wanda Givens spoke from down the hall. She was the head housekeeper at the inn and had worked for Margaret for years. "Are you looking for him?" Wanda pushed her cleaning cart towards us and rattled her key ring.

"Yes Wanda. Dixie Beauregard was found murdered yesterday and we need to speak to Austin immediately. He may know what happened," Cassandra filled her in.

"The nice party planner who was staying here at the inn? Oh my heavens! I can't believe it! Who would want to hurt her?"

"That's what we want to know too," I spoke up.

"Let me give it a try. Housekeeping," she shouted as she banged on the door. She waited a minute before inserting the key and opening the door.

Wanda flipped on the overhead lights and entered the private room leaving her cart in the hallway. She looked around the room and came back to the doorway. "He definitely didn't sleep here last night. His bed is untouched," she informed us. "It doesn't even look like he's been in his room at all since I cleaned yesterday morning."

"What time was that?" Cassandra asked.

"It was early. I'd say around eight. I always started with the party planner group's rooms first since they always left so early. This is just such a tragedy!"

"Where was Dixie's room?" Cassandra questioned the older lady.

"Right next door," Wanda replied as she shut Austin's door behind her and it automatically locked. "She was in room 310. It's the largest suite in the hotel with the sitting room," she elaborated.

"I think the police are probably going to be taking a look around Dixie's room later. I'm surprised they haven't already shown up here," I whispered to Cassandra. I watched as Wanda placed her key in the lock and started opening the door. "Should we stop her?"

"As far as the police are concerned, she was just cleaning the rooms like she always does in the morning. They should have already sent an officer over here to secure her room," she observed.

"You can be so bad," I smacked her arm as Wanda pushed the door open. She entered the opulent suite and turned on the lights. Our ears were assaulted with a blood curdling scream and we rushed behind her to see what was wrong.

"Oh my stars! He's dead!" she screamed as she covered her eyes with her hands and turned away from the bed.

Lying naked in the canopy bed atop scattered red rose petals was Austin, Dixie's assistant and alleged lover. A large knife handle and partial blade stuck out of his chest. His eyes were wide open and glazed. Dark dried blood had pooled beneath his body and spilled onto the white satin duvet. It was hard to estimate how long he had been dead, but from what I could tell, it had been a while judging by the coagulated blood and the rigid appearance of his body.

"How gruesome! We've got to call the police. Amelia, call 911," Cassandra said walking out of the room. "What had Dixie gotten herself into? I cannot believe two people murdered right here in Dogwood Cove. We've got to tell Lincoln!"

"I'm calling him," I informed her as we waited outside the door of Dixie's room, now a crime scene. "Lincoln, tell Detective Mansfield to get over to the Dogwood Inn right away," I shouted into my phone. "Austin is dead and it looks like this has turned into a double murder!"

THIRTEEN

$\mathcal{W}$e were all sitting around the library of the Dogwood Inn. Detective Mansfield and Lincoln had arrived soon after I placed my call. The hallway upstairs was filled with police officers and the coroner had arrived with a gurney. Many of the "pixies" were crying and consoling each other. What started out as a sad day had become exponentially heartbreaking.

Margaret brought out a tea service and handed tea cups filled with a soothing blend of chamomile, peppermint and green tea. We all could use a cup to steady our nerves.

"I've started a pot of coffee if anyone would care for some," Margaret said busying herself by attending to her guests. I was sure her nerves were also unsteady at the discovery of a murder in her establishment. Wanda was a melted puddle of distress, sitting by herself in a winged back chair staring off in the distance. She had become totally distraught after finding Austin dead.

"Who would do something so brutal?" Marcus commented more than asked the room full of co-workers. "Austin was a good guy. I can't believe someone would want to kill him," he said dabbing his eyes with a tissue. The ponytailed Georgia sat next to him on the velvet covered loveseat and put her arm around him giving support.

"Did Austin have any enemies you can think of? Who would benefit from his death?" Detective Mansfield asked the gathered co-workers.

"That's what I'd like to know!" Sam cried. "We were all so close and Austin was a really cool guy. He made working for Dixie bearable," she sniffled and wiped her red rimmed eyes. "I can't believe he's gone!"

"First Dixie, now Austin. Who's next?" Georgia cried as she sipped her tea.

"I don't feel safe being here," another young man added. "There's someone walking around who has killed two of our people. I don't want to sound like an alarmist, but I don't like the odds right now," he adamantly stated. "How do you plan on protecting us, Detective?"

"Calm down, Adam. You'll scare the girls," Marcus warned him.

"Too late! I'm already freaked out!" the redhaired young lady who stayed with Dixie during her plastic surgery spoke up. "I want to get out of here as fast as I can!"

"We are going to have officers in the inn to guard you until our investigation is concluded. None of you are going anywhere. We will find out who did this and we will have you in protective custody in the meantime," he informed them.

"And how long is this going to take? We have lives back in LA you know. We need to get back home and start looking for new jobs," Marcus questioned adjusting his black horn-rimmed glasses. He seemed to speak for the whole group who nodded in agreement.

"I don't want to sound cold. I think I can speak for all of us that we really cared about Austin. But, I don't want to wait around and become the next victim of some psycho who is taking us out one by one. This is starting to remind me of a bad version of *Friday the Thirteenth*, except this is real!" Georgia began crying and was visibly trembling.

"Come here Georgia," Sam urged her. "Come sit next to me. It's going to be all right," she soothed her.

"I know you are all in shock, but pull it together and help give me some leads as to who would want to hurt both Dixie and Austin," Detective Mansfield urged them. "Had there been fighting or arguments with disgruntled vendors? Was anyone suspicious roaming around at the ranch the last few days?"

Everyone sat quietly deep in thought as Cassandra and I looked around the room hoping someone would speak up and provide valuable information.

"Yeah, there was that one dude who was really angry with Dixie. What was his name? You remember?" Adam turned toward Marcus.

"We work with a lot of people Adam. You're going to have to be a little more specific," Marcus replied sarcastically.

"The ice sculptor. What's his name? Something Italian like 'Rigatoni.'"

"You mean John Gambino?" Cassandra questioned. "I've used him for many of our events at Reynolds. He's a true artist."

"That's the guy," Adam confirmed. "He and Dixie had really been in a heated argument this week over the ice sculptures for Olivia's reception."

"Olivia is having ice sculptures? I wasn't aware of that," I commented.

"Dixie had it planned as a surprise. She asked Mr. Gambino to do a sculpture of a horse's head in honor of Maggie

May, but he refused to do it," Georgia explained.

"Why wouldn't he do it?" Cassandra wondered.

"I'm not sure why but he showed up at the barn ranting and raving in Italian," Adam said with his hands in the air mimicking Mr. Gambino's flamboyant gestures. "I don't know what he was saying, but he was angry."

"John can have a temper," I agreed. I personally had seen him upbraid his helper unloading an ice sculpture at the Pink Dogwood Tea Room. The young man had been a bit careless with his cart and John had started yelling at him about being a "worthless knucklehead." I had felt sorry for the worker who seemed humiliated at the loud outburst. I could easily picture him yelling at Dixie.

"Anyone have an idea of what they were arguing about?" Detective Mansfield asked the room? "Maybe artistic differences led to the argument?"

No one answered and they all shook their heads looking perplexed.

"What about Ms. Beauregard's personal life? Jealous boyfriends, ex-husbands? Anyone that might have shown up in town?" the detective pressed on. "We've established she was involved with Austin. Was there anyone else?"

There was an uncomfortable silence in the room as the "pixies" shot looks at each other, obviously keeping quiet about something or someone.

"I know Dixie had an ex-husband," Cassandra volunteered. "I don't remember his name, but apparently he cleaned her out when they went through their divorce. He was awarded a pretty large percentage of her estate."

"Graham Dugan," Marcus stated matter-of-factly. "He and Dixie divorced two years ago. It was quite messy. He got half of Dixie's business holdings and nearly ruined her. That lowlife was nothing but a leech!" he said crossing his arms, disgust written all over his face.

"And how do you know about this?" Mansfield questioned the thin young man.

"I was working for Dixie. She was devastated. She lost about fifteen pounds that year. The stress that man inflicted on her! He was nothing but a glorified househusband and he got a huge cash award. She had to liquidate most of her holdings to settle with him."

"She was an absolute wreck during that time," Georgia agreed. "The divorce was brutal."

"And she became unbearable at work," Adam added. "She was so angry about her divorce, her finances, becoming older. She was not pleasant to be around at all!"

"So true!" Georgia agreed as she twisted her ponytail nervously around her finger. "We all felt terrible for her, but she changed after the divorce."

"Changed how?" Mansfield questioned.

"She became extremely self-conscious about everything from her appearance, to the men she dated, and having everything under control. It couldn't be further from the truth," the redheaded "pixie" weighed in. "I should know since I took care of her for weeks at a time when she had her surgeries. I had to walk Trixie, answer her e-mails, prepare her meals, help her in and out of the bathroom, it was no picnic!"

"Trixie!" Cassandra exclaimed. "Where is Trixie?" she asked as it dawned on her that Dixie's beloved dog was missing.

"She wasn't in her hotel room this morning," Wanda recalled.

"Was she at the barn yesterday?" Cassandra said hopefully.

"Dixie was toting her around as usual. Yes, she was with her all day yesterday," Adam recollected. "Where could Trixie be?"

"Yes, I would like to know that as well," Detective Mansfield agreed. "That dog may be valuable in solving this murder."

FOURTEEN

"There's Lincoln," I pointed to the tall detective standing in the doorway of the library. He motioned for us to follow him. Cassandra and I rose from our chairs and walked behind him into the solarium of the historic inn.

"How's Olivia?" Cassandra asked with concern in her voice. "Is she back at Riverbend Ranch?"

"She just unloaded Jack and she's getting him settled into a stall. He's still spooked. She was glad she stayed with him last night. I want to know how you two got tied into this mess at the inn."

"We came to check on Dixie's people and noticed Austin was missing so we decided to find out where he was," Cassandra said innocently.

"Uh, hmm. And somehow you ended up in Dixie's room?" he said mockingly.

"Wanda was cleaning her room and we heard her scream. We were minding our own business, Lincoln. You believe me, don't you?" she continued.

"I'm not buying it, Cassandra. I know you too well. It wasn't a coincidence that you two were in Dixie's room when Austin's body was discovered."

"Matthew Scott Lincoln. What exactly are you insinuating?" Cassandra played the victim.

"Level with me, OK? What do you know?" he asked sternly.

"We know that Dixie had an ex-husband who benefitted financially from their divorce and that he was a real snake in the grass. We also know that she was arguing with John Gambino at the ranch sometime yesterday afternoon over an ice sculpture he refused to do," I spoke up.

"An ice sculpture?" Lincoln laughed. "Well if Dixie had been killed with a chisel or ice pick I would say we had a suspect. What do you know about this Austin guy? Was he a loner, have any enemies?"

"He not only was Dixie's assistant, but he was intimately involved with her," Cassandra told him.

"That's an interesting twist. Is it possible there was a love triangle of some sort?" he methodically thought aloud.

"It's possible, after what we learned about Dixie from her employees," I speculated.

"I'd say either Austin was involved with someone else or Dixie could have been," Lincoln debated.

"Didn't one of the 'pixies' say something about Austin being upset about one of the ranch hands?" I recalled. "I didn't think anything of it at the time, but it could be a possibility."

"No way. I can't see Dan or the guys even being slightly interested in Dixie. The way she bossed them around, they were practically treated like slaves by her from what Olivia shared with me," Lincoln disputed the idea. "What would attract any one of them to Dixie? They all have wives or girlfriends."

"That doesn't stop a lot of men from cheating," Cassandra mused, "even men who have solid marriages or relationships. If the bait is put out in front of them, they just might bite," she concluded.

I hated to admit it, but Cassandra might be right. Even though I had known the guys at Riverbend Ranch for years, who really knew the private sides to people? It wouldn't be the first time a man had strayed. I was sincerely hoping that this nugget of information was totally wrong.

"There's only one way to get to the bottom of this and that's by hashing this rumor out with the guys. I'm not going to tell Olivia about this until I speak to them myself," Lincoln declared. "She's got enough on her plate right now."

"How's Ruby?" I inquired. "Is she napping, I hope?"

"She didn't get much sleep last night so she's resting. Hopefully, the mothers are steering clear of my little spitfire today. She's not in too good of a mood," he disclosed. "She is eaten up with guilt over what happened to Dixie."

"It wasn't her fault," I reminded him. "Jack had nothing to do with it. There was no way Olivia could have prevented this," I reassured him.

"Please tell me you haven't postponed the wedding." Cassandra pleaded. When he didn't answer right away, she became visibly agitated. "Oh no, this is getting worse by the minute!"

"Olivia is too distraught. I can't see having the wedding tomorrow with everything that has happened," he frowned.

"This is not the end of this discussion," Cassandra said throwing her handbag over her shoulder defiantly.

"Where are you going?" he asked.

"To see your bride and talk some sense into her," she called out as she opened the large front door. "I'll see you back at the ranch."

I followed after her as she unlocked the door to her Mercedes. "We've got one stop on the way to the ranch," she said shifting the car into drive and leaving the bricked driveway of the Dogwood Inn.

"Where are we going?" I wondered.

"To see a man about an ice sculpture!"

"Do you think that's wise? Why not let Lincoln or Detective Mansfield talk with him?" I recommended.

"I have known John for years. If there was a dispute with Dixie, I want to know why. There are a lot of things about Dixie that I'm just learning and I thought I knew her very well," she conceded.

She eased her black German made car in front of Gambino's Creations on West Main Street. It was a few short blocks from the Dogwood Inn. There were no other cars parked in front of the shop so maybe we had lucked out and would be able to speak directly with John.

"Let me do the talking," she suggested. "I have an idea of how to get John to open up about Dixie."

The bell rang on the door as we entered the small shop. I shivered feeling the noticeable drop in temperature I felt upon entering the building. We were soon greeted by the proprietor himself as he walked in from the back of the shop wearing thick insulated gloves and safety glasses.

"Hello, John!" Cassandra called out warmly to the business owner. "How's business? Staying busy?" she shot the bull.

"Mrs. Reynolds! Mrs. Spencer! What a welcome surprise! Business is booming!" he loudly declared and threw his hands up in the air as if he was mimicking a large explosion. "What brings you to my corner of the world?"

"I need an ice sculpture for a fundraising party for my husband. I'm thinking of doing something unique this time. Something custom made."

"Absolutely. I can do anything you want. What did you have in mind?" he asked quizzically placing his hand under his chin.

"Oh, maybe an eagle. Are you good at doing birds and other animals?" she probed.

"Of course. I can make any bird, any animal. No problem!" he assured her.

"John, I hope I'm not prying but I want to ask you a private question."

"Ask away Cassandra. I'm an open book!" he quipped.

"It's about Dixie Beauregard," she dropped the bomb on him.

"What about her?" he asked defensively. He crossed his arms in front of his chest, a definite body language sign of becoming closed off during conversation. I also had noticed an abrupt change in his mood.

"I understand you two had an argument yesterday at Olivia's ranch. What happened?" she pressured the ice artist.

"I'd rather not discuss Ms. Beauregard. As my Mama taught me, if you don't have nothin' nice to say, don't run your mouth," he concluded.

"I guess you haven't heard about Dixie?" she continued undaunted to get to the bottom of her query.

"Heard what?"

"She was murdered yesterday at the ranch," she told him watching his reaction closely.

"Heah. I ain't got nothin' to do with it!" he said putting his hands palms facing us to indicate he was innocent.

"We know that, John. What I want to know is why you were arguing? You may be one of the last people who saw her alive. The police are going to ask you a lot of questions.

I would like to get to the bottom of this so my friend can go on and have a beautiful wedding," she pleaded. "Please, John, help me get some closure for Olivia."

"I feel real bad about not doin' Ms. Rivers's ice sculpture. I had already started workin' on it," he told us.

"So what happened?" Cassandra obliged him to continue.

"I don't want to speak ill of the dead, but her check was bad," he admitted.

"Her check was bad? You've got to be kidding me!" Cassandra exclaimed.

"Yeah, it bounced like rubber! I'm not foolin' ya!" he said in amazement. "She's been bouncin' checks all over town with a lot of people, not just me!"

"What? What in the world could be going on? Olivia wrote her out a very hefty deposit for the vendors and I've already paid Dixie's consulting fees. She had more than enough to cover her expenses," she confirmed.

Oh dear, I thought to myself. This was becoming more bizarre by the moment. Dixie Beauregard had money issues! Cassandra was getting a new view point on her event planner and it was not favorable. First we found out Dixie was a cougar, next that she had extensive plastic surgery and now money issues. What would we find out next? That she was on the "top ten list" on *America's Most Wanted*?

"I was very willing to do Ms. Rivers ice sculpture. As I was sayin,' I already started on it. I just went a little berserk when she wouldn't honor her check. I've got a lot invested in these big blocks of ice. It ain't cheap!" he said picking his teeth with a toothpick.

"And you went out to the ranch to confront Dixie about the check, what did she say?" I bugged him.

"She told me she didn't have any funds available to pay me and she said I could wait to get paid. John Gambino doesn't wait to get paid. I expect half as a deposit and half on delivery. That's pretty standard," he affirmed.

"You and Dixie have done business together for years for the events at Reynolds and my husband's campaign events. Why all the sudden was there a problem?" Cassandra speculated.

"Normally for a good client, I'll allow them to be invoiced for the balance. I'm a fair man," he declared. "But like I said, she's been writing bad checks all over town."

"All over town? Who else has said anything?" I deliberated.

"Floral Fantasies I know for a fact did not have their deposit check clear. Herb is furious with her about it," he told us. "All those sunflowers he special ordered for the wedding. How's he gonna unload those?"

"What? Unbelievable!" Cassandra shouted smacking her hands against her side. "Herb should have called me," she thought aloud. "I would have covered the checks if Dixie was having a cash flow problem," she reported.

"And Herb's not the only one," the burly Italian confided. "The same thing happened with Elegant Edibles. Edna is really steamed because she had already ordered all the produce and supplies. She's out some big bucks. When you own a small business cash flow is so important!"

I knew what John was saying. Having a business was a financial risk and unfortunately, bounced checks from patrons went along with the territory. It was heartbreaking to put together a large tea party, private party or luncheon and find out on Monday the check had bounced. How could people live with themselves knowingly writing bad checks? I had only had that happen a few times and had the issue quickly resolved, but this sounded as if Dixie had not paid her debts.

"How much did she owe you, John?" Cassandra asked taking out her checkbook.

"No, no Mrs. Reynolds. I can't have you do that!"

"I insist. And if I have to go see everyone else this has happened to, I will. I can't have my event planner going about town taking advantage of the businesses in Dogwood Cove. So John, tell me or I'll call your wife and ask. Maria will tell me," Cassandra threatened. And she was right! Maria Gambino was notorious for being a no-nonsense woman. She would tell Cassandra and gladly accept the check.

"You are one heck of a lady, Mrs. Reynolds!" he smiled evidently relieved.

I'd have to agree with him. Cassandra Reynolds was a generous philanthropist and had done much to encourage the arts in Dogwood Cove including serving on the board of the symphony and ballet company. She also had a solid gold heart. Olivia would never know that Cassandra had quietly gone to each vendor and paid them what they were owed. She was not one who wanted credit for what she did behind the scenes. That is why I loved her so much and was so blessed to have her as a friend.

We all were blessed to know Cassandra and just how much we were about to find out!

FIFTEEN

"*I* swear. I didn't touch Austin. He was the one swinging punches at me," an agitated Carl told Lincoln.

"Just what in the heck were you doing messing around with Dixie? I thought you and Sheila were talking about getting engaged," Lincoln reminded the shamed cowboy.

"I've been having second thoughts about Sheila for a while. Things just haven't been good between us," Carl confessed.

"Since Dixie showed up, I'm willing to bet," Lincoln continued grilling the redfaced man. "What were you thinking?"

"Carl, you're one of my strongest guys on the farm. I count on you for everything. I count on you to think before you act. You were left in charge of the barn and feeding the animals. You weren't doing your job if you were in the hayloft with your pants down," Dan publically scolded his ranch hand.

Cassandra and I waited by the barn door listening to the conversation. We didn't want to call any attention to ourselves as we eavesdropped on a humiliating moment for Carl and for all the ranch hands. Life at Riverbend Ranch ran like a well-oiled machine. You were only as strong as your weakest link and Carl had let down the entire group with his carelessness.

"I'm sorry, Dan. It won't happen again," Carl promised.

"Yeah, cause both Dixie and Austin are dead. And that lands you in the hot seat my friend," Lincoln informed him.

Beads of sweat broke out on Carl's forehead and he pushed back his straw cowboy hat to wipe his face with the back of his shirt sleeve. He was looking fretfully around the group of men seated on hay bales in the middle of the barn. He placed his hands on his thighs and began nervously running them up and down.

"I had nothing to do with it, you've got to believe me!" he professed.

"And I would have taken a bullet rather than believe anyone who would have told me you fooled around with Dixie. You've lost all credibility in my book," Dan informed him. "Sheila is my wife's sister. She's family. If you need to move on at least have the guts to tell her before you start something up with someone new."

"It wasn't like that; I didn't realize what was happening. She kind of threw herself at me," Carl stammered. "I was upstairs throwing the hay bales down when she came up behind me. It happened real fast! I never wanted to hurt Sheila. I swear, Dan!"

"So you were unaware that Dixie was interested in you up until that point? There were no conversations between the two of you? No flirtatious comments? She just seduced you and you were unable to defend yourself, right?" Lincoln asked mercilessly.

"I know how it sounds. But it happened so fast I hardly had time to think," he said defensively. "I was minding my own business and then she was behind me, rubbing my back. I know it sounds strange, but that's how it happened."

"And let me guess, you just couldn't say no!" Dan laughed. "Sorry, bud but you're up the creek without a paddle."

"So, let's skip ahead to what happened next. Spare us the gory details, but when did the confrontation occur with Austin?" Lincoln continued the inquisition.

"We were fooling around, umm" he paused clearing his throat, "and then Austin was grabbing me and started pushing me around like he was going to push me right out of the loft. I had to hit him to get him off me," he stated. "Then Dixie started hitting Austin in the back and told him to stop."

"And where was everyone else?" Lincoln interrupted.

"They were working downstairs in the barn. They started yelling up to see what was going on," he recounted his humiliation.

"And then what happened? This should be good," Dan chuckled.

"Dixie got him to calm down and I got out of there as fast as I could. I didn't want any part of that," he sheepishly admitted.

"Was that the last time you saw Dixie?" Lincoln inquired.

"Yeah. I went down by the corral after that and waited for everybody to get back from the trail ride. I saw her workers start pulling out around four-thirty or so. I just lay low," he concluded.

"Did you see Dixie leave?"

"I thought I did. I saw her Land Rover drive through the gates about fifteen minutes later. I assumed she was gone," Carl said.

"You are in quite a pickle," Dan shook his head. "Why didn't you come to me and tell me all this when Dixie was found murdered. Did you really think no one would report the fight when there was a barn full of witnesses?"

"I didn't want Sheila to find out. It was a mistake and I didn't want to hurt her," Carl admitted. "She doesn't deserve that."

"No she doesn't deserve that and you are going to tell her," Dan told him. "I've got to go home to my wife later today and I will not have her angry at me that I knew. You two-timed my sister-in-law. You're going to have to face the music, my friend."

"I'm sorry, Dan. I'm sorry, Lincoln! I don't know what got into me? I guess I was just flattered she was interested in me. I don't know!" he shouted.

"Sounds like she played you like a violin. I'm willing to bet this was some sort of ploy to get Austin jealous. Why else would she do it in such a public place as a barn full of her workers and her boyfriend?" Lincoln speculated.

"She used me? Is that what you're saying?" Carl said bewildered. "Why would she do that?"

"My young friend, why do women do half the things they do? I think it's to keep men off balance," Lincoln grinned. "I'd say she got the reaction she wanted out of Austin. You just happened to be in the wrong place at the wrong time."

"And I've screwed everything up with Sheila over it. How could I have been so stupid?"

"This isn't over Carl," Dan scowled. "You've compromised your position at the ranch. We're going to have to talk with Olivia and let her decide how she wants to handle this indiscretion."

"Look, Dan. Dixie and I just messed around. We didn't actually *do* anything, if you get my drift," he divulged. "You've got to believe me."

"You still need to tell Sheila. She deserves to know," Dan said seriously.

"I will. I'll tell her tonight," Carl promised.

"I think you better show up with flowers for your wife," Lincoln joked with Dan.

"Yeah. She's going to be upset about this. But hey, I didn't know!" Dan reasoned.

"And I don't think there's a big enough bouquet of flowers in town to save your butt, Carl!" Lincoln jested with his shaken friend. "You screwed the pooch on this one, bud!"

"If you guys are done with your brotherly love fest, I've got some things I'd like to discuss with you," Cassandra announced walking through the door. The men immediately grew quiet and looked shocked. "Carl, I'd like to begin with you…"

SIXTEEN

"Oh you're here, Sarah! Good!" I called out to my friend in the driveway as she pulled up in her Smart Car.

"I came as soon as I got your message. What's up?"

"How was the tea room today?" I said welcoming her with a hug.

"I don't know. I took the day off," she smiled and tossed her hair back. I knew that look! Sarah McCaffrey had a love interest and I was willing to bet it was Tom Lincoln.

"Oh," I said nonchalantly. "So what did you do all day?"

"I showed Tom around Dogwood Cove and then we had a little picnic out at Abrams Falls. It was a beautiful afternoon!" she sighed and floated next to me.

Oh, dear. Sarah was head-over-heels and it was written plain as day all over her face. I hoped there would be mutual feelings. She was such a wonderful person. A bit naïve and gullible, but that's what we all loved about her, her innocence and goodness. I was not about to burst her bubble.

"Speaking of Tom, where is he?" I asked as our shoes crunched on gravel.

"He's at the General Morgan Inn with his parents. They are going to come over in a little while. They wanted to let

Olivia and Ruby get some uninterrupted rest today," she reported. Her smile beamed brighter than a toothpaste commercial. She was smitten!

"There are some things you need to know before we go inside," I stopped her before we got any closer to the door. "They found Austin murdered at the Dogwood Inn this morning."

"What? Oh dear? What happened?" she gasped.

"He had been stabbed in the chest with a large knife. And it gets worse," I paused.

"What, Amelia? Tell me?" she pleaded.

"Austin had been in a fight with Carl at the barn during the trail ride. That makes him a suspect," I informed her.

"He was fighting with Carl? Why?" she said still shocked.

"Carl and Dixie were messing around in the hayloft. Austin caught them together and went into a crazy rage because he was secretely involved with Dixie. But Olivia doesn't know all this yet, so you can't tell her. It would devastate her right now."

"That little skunk! I can't believe Carl would cheat on Sheila. What is wrong with him?" Sarah exclaimed. "She's a wonderful lady. He's lucky to have her."

"Well, I think the luck has run out for Carl. Lincoln had to take him down to the station to sign a statement as to what happened," I said glumly.

"Poor, Olivia! Now she will have to worry about Carl and what will happen to him. What else could possibly go wrong?" Sarah sighed.

"That is why I called you. We've got to have a bridal intervention and get our friend out of her funk. Cassandra is inside with her now. It's going to take all of us to convince her to move forward with the wedding," I said encouragingly.

"I'll do anything I can to help. After all, I am a hopeless romantic," she smiled and squeezed my hand as we walked into the warm kitchen. Grandmother Laurel was busy peeling potatoes over the farmhouse sink while Cassandra sat at the long table speaking earnestly to Olivia.

"Honey, people have traveled and made arrangements to be here for the wedding. Think of how disappointed they will be if you don't have the ceremony. I know Dixie would want you to move forward with the wedding. She was a consummate professional," Cassandra lied and shot a look of conspiracy in my direction.

I nodded my head in agreement and walked up to the table.

"Liv, the best to way to put all this to rest is to move on and what better way to spread happiness than to have a wedding?" I suggested hugging my redhaired friend from behind. She was wearing a flannel robe and slippers, a rare sight on this woman who was up before dawn feeding her animals and working up to the last minute at night to get all the chores done. She must be in a depression if she was dragging around in a robe.

"How can I move on? Dixie was killed in my barn, the very spot where my reception was going to be held. I think it's a bit morbid to just forget all that and have the wedding. I just can't do that. It's not right," she argued.

"Have you talked with Lincoln about this?" I asked. "What does he think?"

"He said it's up to me. I don't know. I'm just starting to think it's a sign that maybe this whole marriage thing is a bad idea," she said as she began crying.

"You have the jitters, my sweet girl," Grandmother Laurel said as she came over to her granddaughter and began petting her hair. "I can remember feeling that way the night before my wedding to your grandfather. I was petrified!" the wise woman shared.

"You were?" Olivia asked incredulously. "But you and Granddad loved each other so much!"

"Yes we did and I always will love him. I miss him every day! But that didn't stop me from being nervous," she confessed as Olivia dried her eyes and faced Laurel.

"But you didn't have someone die right before your wedding. This is different," Olivia shook her head. "It's a sign that Lincoln and I don't belong together."

"That's sheer nonsense!" Ruby Rivers spoke up from the hallway. "I've seen how that man looks at you. You better marry him tomorrow or I'll tan your hide!" she threatened.

"Mama, what are you doing out of bed?" Olivia fussed. "You hardly slept!"

"There's time for sleep later. I want to see how my only daughter is doing," Ruby said lovingly moving over to the table and taking a seat. "This has been a nightmare for you, I know, but Lincoln and Detective Mansfield will find out who did this and then you can relax."

"Precisely my point, we don't know who killed Dixie and now Austin. I'm having a hard time justifying having the wedding tomorrow with a killer on the loose," Olivia acknowledged.

"Tragedies happen every day. That's why you've got to hold on to happiness when you have it. Life is uncertain. If anything, take that away from Dixie's death. Marry Lincoln tomorrow," Cassandra urged her best friend.

"What is this? An intervention?" Olivia laughed looking around the kitchen at the women who were there offering support. "Am I that bad?"

"Difficult is a more appropriate term I think," Cassandra joked. "Don't screw things up with Lincoln."

"Yes. Don't screw things up with my son," Audrey Lincoln smiled and joined the group. "If you do, I will never forgive you breaking my son's heart."

"Oh, Audrey! I don't want to break Lincoln's heart. There's just been too much that's happened!" Olivia explained to her future mother-in-law.

"Let Matt handle the investigation. That's his job. You're right. So much has happened and I am determined that there will be a wedding tomorrow. You and Matt have a wonderful supportive group of friends and family who want to make sure that you two have a beautiful day tomorrow. Now, if we can get the bride on board!"

"Thank you, everyone! Thank you!" Olivia said openly weeping. "I'm sorry I'm so emotional these days," she said going around the room and hugging everyone.

"Did you come all this way by yourself Audrey?" Ruby asked.

"No. Lewis and Tom are out in the barn with Dan and the ranch hands. They've got a little bachelor party cooked up for Matt as soon as he gets here," she reported.

"A bachelor party! Wonderful!" Cassandra commented.

"We might as well have a bachelorette party since we are all gathered."

"Lincoln isn't here? Where is he?" Olivia said sounding worried.

"I'm sure he's working on the case. Don't you fret our little bride-to-be. He will be here soon."

"What's going on that I don't know about?" Olivia confronted the group. "Out with it!"

"Everything's fine honey. Lincoln is down at the station taking a statement. He won't be long," Cassandra attempted to reassure her high-strung friend.

"Questioning who? Do they have a lead?" she said hopefully.

"Everything is fine. He'll be here soon!" Cassandra said again.

"I heard you the first time and you ignored my question. I know you aren't good at lying to me, so you are holding something back. I want to know what the heck is going on around here!" she shouted.

"Calm down Liv. It won't do any good to get worked up," I said in a low monotone voice. "Lincoln doesn't have a suspect. He's taking a statement."

"A statement sounds like someone is under investigation. Who is it? Tell me!"

"It's Carl!" Sarah cracked. "He had a fight with Austin in the barn."

"Loose lips sink ships, Sarah! I told you to keep quiet," I reminded her.

"She knows something's up. Better to not keep secrets," Sarah replied.

"Thank you for telling me the truth, Sarah. Now what in the world happened between Austin and Carl? And I want the uncut version."

"Carl was fooling around with Dixie in the hayloft. Nothing really happened between them, but Austin caught them and there was a scuffle," I told her.

"And now Carl is giving the police his statement," Cassandra continued. "Lincoln took him in as soon as he found out about the fight."

"Why didn't he tell me himself? Why all the secrets?" Olivia demanded.

"He knew you would be upset about Carl. He thought he would spare you and get it all resolved without worrying you," Cassandra said.

"I need to know what is going on at my ranch at all times. I don't need someone else trying to be a buffer and keep things from me. When I get a hold of Carl, I'm going to wring his little neck! What was he thinking fooling around with Dixie? He knows better!" Olivia fumed as she rose from the table.

"Where are you going?" Ruby called as Olivia walked down the hall.

"To put my clothes on and talk with Dan. I'm going to get to the bottom of this!" she declared as she continued down the hallway.

SEVENTEEN

"*W*here's Lincoln?" Olivia demanded as she walked through the crowded room of work stations and approached Detective Mansfield. He seemed to be surprised to see Olivia with Cassandra and myself in tow.

"What are you ladies doing here today? I thought you would be knee deep in wedding preparations," he remarked as he rose from his desk and greeted us.

"Will you let Lincoln know I am here? I need to speak to him right away," Olivia stated to the confused detective.

"He's in the interrogation room right now. I'll let him know you're here when he gets a break. Would you like to wait over there?" he recommended gesturing to the waiting area.

"Sure, we'll wait. Thank you," Cassandra smiled as Olivia stomped off into the well-used lobby area. She plunked herself down in a plastic molded chair and began tapping her boots with impatience.

"You're going to drive me crazy if you keep up that noise. You're practically shaking the floor!" Cassandra complained putting her hand on Olivia's leg to stop the constant movement.

"I'm just so mad at Lincoln and Carl right now. I don't know which one I'd like to take out to the whipping post first! How dare he keep this from me? I need to know what's going on at *my ranch!*"

"Calm down, Liv!" I implored my high-strung friend. "There is so much going on right now. Lincoln was just trying to take some of the stress off of you and lighten your burden. He is a cop after all, and he can be a great help right now," I reminded her.

Cassandra had insisted on driving Olivia to the police station due to her emotional state after the scene we had witnessed in the barn when she had confronted Dan and Bill. Suffice it to say, Dan was reminded that his employer had a temper and that all ranch business should be brought to her attention first, husband or no husband!

Sarah had decided to stay behind to act as hostess to the Lincolns and didn't seem to mind looking after Tom and his parents. Ruby and Laurel had also remained at Riverbend Ranch to spend time getting to know their soon to be in-laws better and after a stern lecture from Olivia, we were confident Ruby would behave.

"He knows better than to interfere in how I handle my ranch hands. How does it look to Dan, Bill and Carl that he went behind my back and didn't tell me what was going on at my own ranch? That's my business. I started it, I have built it from the ground up and I'm not going to have the guys go to Lincoln when there is a problem and cut me out of the equation altogether. It usurps my authority!"

I could see her point. When you're a woman in business, especially a business that is usually run by men, it's hard to earn respect. Cassandra knew firsthand how hard it was to run a corporation and break through the "boy's club." Olivia had fought tooth and nail not only to grow a successful therapeutic horseback riding center, but to garner the admiration of her ranch hands. She had achieved both.

"What are you doing here, Herb?" Cassandra asked the pudgy owner of Floral Fantasies as he came in and sat in the waiting area.

"I'm being questioned in the Dixie Beauregard murder," he said looking rather nervous. He adjusted the collar of his lilac dress shirt and waved his hand to circulate air around his face. "I can't believe all this. It's become a personal nightmare for me."

"Why would the police want to talk to you?" Olivia asked bewildered. "She was killed at my ranch. What do you have to do with it?"

"I was contracted with Dixie for the flowers for your wedding," Herb explained. "They've been questioning all the wedding vendors this morning. Edna called me to tell me she's already been down here twice. Her nerves are shot, that's for sure!" he informed us as he smoothed the crease in his lime green and purple plaid pants.

"Edna from Elegant Edibles has been questioned? Are they searching for a needle in a haystack or do they just not have any solid leads?" Olivia thought aloud.

"It's about her money issues. It's always about the money, money, money!" he exclaimed as fidgeted in his chair.

"Money issues? What money issues?"

"Um, Herb. Would you like to take a walk with me to the vending area?" Cassandra interrupted and jumped up from her chair. She grabbed Herb's arm and pulled him abruptly from his seat. "I'm sure Olivia will need something to munch on while we wait. We'll be right back. You stay put!" she told us as she dragged a befuddled Herb along the hallway.

"How long has she been acting like this?" Olivia turned to question me.

"She seems fine to me," I said with a straight face.

"What's this money business Herb is talking about?" she continued.

"I don't know anything about Herb's business. How well do we really know anyone?" I mused aloud hoping to throw Olivia off.

"Edna has been here two times today? What do they think happened? They quarreled over which cheese to pair with which wine? She killed her with a corkscrew? This is ridiculous. The police need to be spending their time looking for the real murderer. I've known Edna and Herb for years. There is no way they had anything to do with Dixie's murder," she said emphatically.

"Hey, ladies!" John Gambino greeted us as he took a chair.

"Hi John," I said nervously pulling out my cell phone. I decided to send Cassandra a text reading "SOS, ice man in the house!"

"How are you John?" Olivia asked the large man who took up almost two chairs with his muscular build.

"I'll be much better once this Dixie business is resolved and behind me, rest in peace," he said referring to the deceased.

"What Dixie business are you talking about John?" Olivia asked. "First Herb, then Edna, now you. I wasn't aware you knew my wedding planner."

"Oh, you know John did a lot of work with Dixie during Doug's campaign," I interjected shooting John a direct look. "I'm sure the police are questioning everyone Dixie knew here in town looking for leads, isn't that right John?"

"Yes, Amelia. It's routine questioning, I'm sure. I'm so sorry this happened at your ranch, Olivia. You doin OK?" he asked as he patted Olivia's shoulder.

"I'm hanging in there John. I'm waiting to talk to Lincoln and find out what the police know," she explained.

I exchanged knowing glances with Cassandra and Herb as they approached our trio. It was obvious to me that Cassandra had spoken to Herb and asked him to withhold his information about Dixie's bad checks. He tried his best to appear nonchalant, but had an almost comical look on his face. Herb was not a good actor.

"Hello, John! So nice to see you. It's been ages! How's Maria?" Cassandra babbled with the brawny ice sculptor.

"She's doin' great, Cassandra," John joined in the charade. "How ya been? Can we expect Mr. Reynolds to run for Senate soon?"

"Funny you should mention that, John. We were just talking about that and I think he will be making a decision in the next few weeks. Thanks for asking."

"So Herb, I've been meaning to talk with you about doing a workshop for the Dogwood Ladies Guild on the meaning of flowers and herbs during the Victorian era," I said joining the diversion.

"I would love to do a workshop on that subject! When and where are you planning this?" he asked lifting his eyebrows up in feigned interest.

"There you are Lincoln!" Olivia jumped up as the tall detective advanced towards his fiancée, an embarrassed Carl following behind. "I want to know what's going on here, Carl!"

"I can explain," Carl stammered as he looked down at his

tiny employer who was standing at her full height of five feet and looking dangerously close to decking him.

"Calm down, Liv," Lincoln attempted to intervene.

"Don't tell me to calm down. I'm furious with both of you. You should have come to me first or talked to Dan," Olivia chastised. "And you shouldn't have kept this from me, Lincoln!"

"It's not his fault, Olivia. Please don't be angry with Matt. I didn't tell anyone because I was afraid of losing my job. I don't know what I was thinking!"

"You know I have strict rules about fraternizing with the clients," Olivia continued.

"I know. I'm so sorry! Truly I am. And now I've got to tell Sheila. She's going to be devastated," Carl said sounding totally downtrodden.

"I hope she was worth it, Carl. Of all the women out there, Dixie Beauregard? I don't understand!" Olivia said puzzled. "I wouldn't think she was your type, Carl."

"She's not. It just happened. I wasn't thinking and I swear, it will never happen again. She was using me, Olivia, to make Austin jealous. That's all it was!"

"Make Austin jealous? Is she the reason Austin was murdered?" Olivia questioned her groom-to-be. "Next we'll hear Dixie was fooling around with Herb and John," she said sarcastically.

"Don't be lookin' at me. She aint my type," John Gambino said shaking his head emphatically. "If Maria heard you say that, I'd be out on my ear!"

"She's definitely not my type," Herb quickly added. "I maintain professional relationships with all my clients," he explained.

"So why are they down here?" Olivia asked Lincoln. "And why was Edna from Elegant Edibles questioned twice today. I want to know what is going on!"

"I think I better head back to the ranch if I'm done here," Carl said meekly in Olivia's direction.

"We'll talk more later Carl. See you back at the ranch." She was not done with him yet and would probably give him a good chewing out, but not here in front of everyone else. She would have to re-establish her authority with him if he were going to stay on at Riverbend Ranch, that much I was certain.

"You better sit down, Liv. There was a lot about Dixie that none of us knew," he told her as he gently guided her down in a chair. "I didn't want to involve you with all the wedding plans up in the air and the stress you've been under for a while now."

"I know you meant well, Lincoln, but I don't operate that way. I believe in total honesty at all times. I need to know what's been going on right under my nose. I think I deserve to know and I assure you I can handle it," she concluded.

"Herb, if you will follow me," Detective Mansfield said flatly as he escorted a jittery Herb to the interrogation room.

"Call me if you need me Herb," Cassandra yelled as he waved to us. I could see perspiration marks appearing on his dress shirt. He looked a bit peaked.

"Mr. Gambino, if you'll follow me," Detective Schwartz, a co-worker of Lincoln's, requested.

"I'll see you ladies later," John Gambino said as he followed behind Schwartz.

"So why are all my wedding vendors being questioned?" Olivia asked point blank. "Do you think one of them had motive to kill Dixie?"

"Money can make people do crazy things," Lincoln indicated. "Dixie owed a lot of people a lot of money."

"What? Are you saying she owed money to Herb?"

"Yes and to several other businesses around town," he told her.

"How many other businesses are we talking about?" she asked as she looked around at Cassandra and me. "Did you know about this?" she asked us.

"I just found out this morning Olivia," Cassandra admitted. "I didn't want to upset you with everything that has been going on this week with the wedding."

"But I paid her upfront for all the deposits and just two days ago I paid her the balance on all the accounts," she divulged. "This isn't making any sense. Everyone should have been paid. So where is the money?"

"I don't know," Cassandra informed her.

"That's what we are trying to find out. We've been looking over her financial records and have been in touch with her bank in California. Olivia, Dixie was in debt way over her head. She owed a lot of people money, not just here in Dogwood Cove but in LA, New York, wherever she was hired to do events. She was in pretty deep and has left a significant paper trail," Lincoln reported.

"Oh my gosh! I had no idea!" Cassandra said shaking her head and putting her hands over her eyes. "I've known Dixie for years and this is not like her."

"And there's more. She was burned pretty badly in her divorce a few years ago," he continued.

"That's who you should interview, her ex-husband. He has the most to gain with her death," Cassandra shouted.

"Don't go jumping to conclusions. We've already had the

LA police bring him in for questioning. He has a solid alibi. He hasn't heard from Dixie for months. He did shed some light on some of her recent business dealings and we are following some leads he gave us," he said.

"What kind of leads?" Olivia questioned him.

"Well, her ex-husband told us that she had a silent business partner who had invested heavily in Dixie's business following the divorce. He wasn't sure who that individual was but we're hoping to find something in Dixie's personal belongings or loan papers from her bank that will give us his or her name," he finished.

"You mentioned personal belongings. Dixie always carried her day planner with her. Maybe there would be a clue as to who this mystery investor is in her day planner," Cassandra said enthusiastically.

"We didn't find it on her person, her Land Rover or in her hotel room," he disclosed. "I think if we find her day planner, we'll find our perp."

"What about a laptop?" I suggested. "I have all my business contacts listed in my hard drive."

"We located her laptop in her Land Rover. We've got our tech team taking a look at it right now. I can tell you there were some scathing e-mails," he said seriously.

"What do you mean by 'scathing?'" Cassandra looked up with concern in her voice.

"Threatening e-mails about money she owed. Like I said, Dogwood Cove was not the only community where she had outstanding debt. She was behind on all of her bills, some more than nine months. There were a lot of ticked off people who had not been paid for work completed months before."

"Oh goodness! Where was all her money going?" Olivia wondered.

"We learned she was having multiple plastic surgery procedures," I spoke up. "And didn't Marcus mention traveling to Las Vegas with Austin on several trips?" I asked Cassandra.

"Yes, he did mention that. That just made me think, Amelia…"

"Think what?" I asked.

"You don't think she had a problem with . . . no she wouldn't have," she turned away and looked out the window.

"Wouldn't have what, Cassandra?" Olivia implored trying to get her dear friend to complete her thought. "Just say it! We might all be thinking it anyway."

"Do you think she had a gambling problem? I hate to say it and I could be wrong. But what else do you go to Las Vegas to do?" she asked us.

"I could care less about the casinos. I would go for the buffets," Olivia stated. She was always all about the food, though she had not been lately with the stress of the wedding.

"Maybe she liked the shows? Who knows? It's like the commercials, 'what goes on in Vegas stays in Vegas,'" I suggested.

"Unless you are a murder victim," Lincoln said excitedly. "Thank you ladies! I think we have a new lead," he jumped up and started walking towards his work station.

"What lead? What are you talking about?" Olivia quickly asked following Lincoln.

"Let me get back to work. I'll call you when I know something more definite," he stopped as he planted a kiss atop her auburn head. "It's going to be a long day, but I'm determined to find who killed Dixie and Austin."

"I just love that man," Cassandra said sighing. "He has this hard edge to him that I find most attractive. I wish Doug were more like that," she said shaking her head as if in a daze.

"Back off sister. He's mine!" Olivia joked.

"Speaking of Doug, did he make it back the other night? With all the chaos, I forgot to ask," I admitted.

"He's back but just for the weekend. He will be sure to be at the wedding tomorrow," she informed us.

"Wedding tomorrow? Are you kidding? My wedding planner is dead, my reception site is a crime scene, my groom is working over-time to find the killer, my mother is driving me crazy, I haven't had any sleep in two days and you want me to be a radiant bride by tomorrow? No way, no can do!"

"You focus on getting some sleep and leave everything else to us," Cassandra told her headstrong girlfriend.

"How can I get married tomorrow knowing Dixie and Austin's killer is on the loose?"

"Let Lincoln handle the case. We've got work to do, but first, that bachelorette party you didn't have last night. Come with me!" Cassandra said and dragged a protesting Olivia out to her Mercedes.

"Bachelorette party? Oh, Cassandra. I don't want a stripper!" Olivia whined.

"Who said anything about strippers? Get your head out of the gutter and be prepared to enjoy yourself!" she said as she stepped on the gas pedal and eased back on Main Street.

EIGHTEEN

"This was such a great idea!" Olivia said as we sipped champagne in the dry heat sauna. We were enjoying the amenities at the Austin Springs Spa in the Carnegie Hotel. Wrapped in plush white terry robes, we inhaled the warm air and felt our muscles relax.

"This cucumber water is so refreshing," Audrey said exhaling deeply. "I never would have thought to add sliced cucumber to my water. I will have to try this at my next garden party."

"Oh, you must have a beautiful garden," Ruby commented. "A garden party sounds lovely."

"You and Laurel will have to come for a visit at Christmas. I would love to show you around Dallas," Lincoln's mom said excitedly. "We could shop at The Galleria and go to the Ft. Worth Stock Yards."

"That sounds like fun. I would love to visit," Ruby agreed.

I was happy for Olivia that the mothers had put down the swords and were bonding. I think Cassandra had impressed Audrey and bridged the gap between the two families. I was finding myself amused with the mothers making plans for a visit for the holidays.

"Don't you think that would be nice?" Ruby asked Olivia who was sitting up with her eyes closed.

"What? I'm sorry, I didn't hear you," Olivia said opening her puffy blood shot eyes.

"Audrey invited us to come to Dallas for Christmas. Wouldn't that be nice to celebrate the holidays in Texas?" Ruby said patting Olivia on the knee.

"Sure. That sounds nice," she said yawning loudly. "We could string lights on a cactus." At least she still had her sense of humor.

"Ladies, who is next for their Swedish massage?" a young spa attendant asked as she peeked her head into the sauna.

"Why don't you head over to the massage suite now and maybe you can catch a few winks during your treatment," I suggested to Olivia.

"That would be nice. I think I will take you up on your offer," she agreed slowly standing up and following the spa attendant down the dimly lit hallway.

"I think I've had enough of the sauna. Is there somewhere we can go while we are waiting for our pedicure appointments?" Audrey asked.

"Follow me," Sarah said leading the way to the lounge area.

I loved coming to the Austin Springs Spa because of its relaxing atmosphere and attention to detail. When you entered the treatment area, the lights were dim and candles flickered along the walls while the trickling sounds from the fountain greeted you. Seating areas with plush leather sofas were scattered about.

Many patrons took advantage of the time between spa treatments to relax and stay warm with a neck wrap and soft blanket while they sipped on lemon or cucumber water. A gift card from the spa was my favorite present to receive for any occasion and the girls and I had spent many wonderful relaxing hours here together.

"I can't believe my little girl is getting married tomorrow," Ruby said as her eyes misted with tears. "This is a very happy day for our family. Chris would have been so proud to give her away. I wish he were here to see this."

"He's with us in spirit, honey," Laurel said patting her daughter-in-law's hand in a comforting show of affection. "He would have loved having Matt as a son-in-law."

"Thank you for saying that, Laurel," Audrey Lincoln replied. "This is a very happy occasion for our family as well. They say when your son marries, you lose a son. I'm hoping that I've gained a daughter. We could use some estrogen in our family!"

"Would anyone else care for more cucumber water while you are waiting?" the spa attendant asked our group. "It shouldn't be too much longer before your next appointments."

"I would love some more water. Anyone else?" Sarah asked.

"I think we all are a bit parched after the sauna," Cassandra spoke up.

"I'll help Tina and be right back," Sarah softly spoke keeping her voice down so as not to disturb the other spa clients.

"I love that girl," Laurel smiled as she watched Sarah. "She has a big heart and warm spirit. Some man will be lucky to snag her."

"You could not be more right," I agreed with Laurel. Sarah was one-of-a-kind and had done so much to help with Olivia's wedding from the thoughtful tea shower to the kissing balls she had hand crafted for tomorrow's event. We were all very excited to pull the festivities together and surprise Olivia.

"While our bride is preoccupied, let's go over what we have left to do for tomorrow," Cassandra said in a conspirator's whisper. "I'm working with Marcus and the 'pixies' on getting the tent raised. If we can keep Olivia busy until sundown, we may be able to drive her home without her seeing the event area."

"How are we going to do that?" Ruby questioned. "She has an eye like a hawk!"

"While our little cowgirl is worn out and my thoughts are to give her a 'spa-tini' cocktail after her massage and she will most likely snooze all the way home. I've told Marcus I'll call when we start to head to the ranch so he and the team can kill the lights until we have Olivia safely in the farmhouse."

"She's going to be so surprised, Cassandra!" Sarah added as she handed out fresh glasses of water to everyone. "Are we going to start decorating tonight?"

"Marcus has large flood lights plugged in so we can decorate tonight and have everything ready for tomorrow," I explained. "Dan, Bill and Carl are already at the reception site lending a hand so we will have extra 'man power' should we need it."

"You don't think Olivia will notice all the activity?" Ruby asked skeptically.

"The farmhouse sits on the far side of the property. Once we get past the front pasture where the tent is staked, we're home free. She can't see the pasture from her house and I'm willing to bet she will go right to sleep," Cassandra plotted.

"You girls have thought of everything. Olivia is so fortunate to have friends like you. What can I do to help decorate?" Audrey volunteered. "You know I've headed up many fundraising events and party organization is one of my many strong suits!"

"I'm glad to hear you say so, Audrey!" Cassandra grinned. "We could use help directing the rental company on where to set up the tables, chairs, and dance floor. I have a schematic drawn up for the tent. They shouldn't have any problem following it, but I would feel better having someone in charge of the unloading and setting up."

"I can do it. Check it off!" Audrey clapped her hands together eagerly. "And be sure to put Tom and Lewis to work. We don't have slackers in my family."

"Tom and Lewis can help Dan and the ranch hands lay down the dance floor so we can get this done fast."

"Shane and I will place the pumpkin topiaries and curly willow arches and lights around the tent. He's already loaded them up at the barn."

"Marcus and the crew are going to light the tent and begin the transformation. They are prepared to be there all night if they have to," Cassandra declared. "They are insistent that Olivia's wedding should be one of their best affairs to honor Dixie and Austin's memory."

"How wonderful and kind of all of them," Sarah said dabbing her eyes with a tissue she pulled from her robe pocket. "I think Olivia and Lincoln will be so surprised."

"Is there anything else I'm forgetting?" Cassandra asked.

"Floral Fantasies will come out in the morning and place the table centerpieces, right?" I reminded her.

"Yes. And Elegant Edibles will set up around ten AM

while we are at Armando's having our hair and makeup done for the event," Cassandra replied. "We are going to get dressed at the farmhouse, so everyone make sure you have your dresses with you in the morning as well as shoes, handbags, jewelry, etc."

"Are you sure you haven't organized a wedding before?" Audrey teased. "With your skills, you could run a large corporation!" she joked.

"I have thrown quite a few parties, I have to admit. But this one is going to be special. I don't want anything ruining Olivia's big day. She deserves it," Cassandra said as her voice warbled.

"Oh no! I've got tissues!" Sarah said as she began passing them to the group. "We can't start crying now. There's plenty of time for that tomorrow!" she said blowing her nose.

"Ladies, would you care for some 'spa-tinis?'" the young spa attendant asked as she passed filled martini glasses to everyone. "It's not a bachelorette party without a cocktail!"

"Oh wonderful!" Laurel said as she was presented with her glass. "The bride is having her massage. I hate for her to miss the cocktails."

"What am I missing?" Olivia interjected as she joined us on the oversized leather sofa.

"Oh good! We were just getting ready for a 'spa-tini!'" Audrey told her. "Now that the bride is here, we can toast! To Olivia and Matt. May you have many happy years together. Welcome to our family!"

"To Olivia and Lincoln," we all joined in and clinked glasses.

"And a toast to 'The Traveling Tea Ladies!' To the best friends a girl could ever have!" Olivia beamed with delight.

NINETEEN

"Perfect. Thanks, Dan! The dance floor is finished," Cassandra called out enthusiastically to the crowd busily working. The "pixies" were up on a cherry picker attaching curly willow boughs wrapped in white twinkle lights to the ceiling of the enormous tent. Each of us was wearing an ear bud and radio and had become unofficial "pixies" for the evening.

"What's next, Cassandra?" Dan inquired.

"Is the carriage ready to go for tomorrow?" she quickly consulted her clipboard. She had taken over Dixie's role quite well, though she had some big shoes to fill. The carriage had been the perfect solution to Olivia's concerns about getting on and off Maggie May in her wedding gown.

"Carl is at the barn polishing the carriage and tack," the foreman reported.

"Why don't you take a dinner break if you haven't already? I'm sure you've worked up an appetite," Cassandra suggested patting Dan on the back. He was devoted to the ranch and kept things running smoothly. He was irreplaceable and Olivia was lucky to have him as her right hand.

"I think dinner sounds like a great idea," he agreed walking over to where Sarah was handing out paper plates mounded with Philly cheese steak sandwiches dripping with sautéed green peppers and onions. She handed Dan an ice cold beer and helped him grab a seat at a nearby table.

"Thanks, Sarah," Dan said tipping his hat. "You ladies have sure worked hard. It's going to be a great wedding," the man of few words said.

"We could not have done it without all your help, Dan!" Sarah smiled and hurried back to make another plate for Bill. "Where's Carl?" she asked the ranch hand.

"Making sure the carriage is polished and in perfect running order. It's going to be a beautiful day according to the weather man," Bill answered as he accepted his overflowing plate.

Shane and I were busy unloading the topiaries at each of the tent's four entrances. The large metal urns had an aged green patina finish and each held a trio of white pumpkins in graduated sizes with the smallest at the top. Marcus had carefully drilled small holes in each of the pumpkins and pushed white twinkling lights through them. The effect was sheer elegance. Everything was coming together beautifully.

"OK, Sam. Lower that light just a tad more," Marcus called out to his spikey haired co-worker. "OK, stop right there. That looks great!"

And it did. The entire tent was decorated with various bulbs and glass containers filled with candles dangling from the lit curly willow branches suspended from the ceiling. The lights were low enough to hang just above each of the sixteen foot tables lining the room. It gave intimacy and coziness to the large reception area. The effect was breathtaking.

"Oh, Marcus! Wait until we top these tables tomorrow with Herb's centerpieces. This is stunning!" Cassandra complimented the head 'pixie.' "You must consider going into business for yourself. You definitely have an eye for drama and style," she said with authority. And she should know. She was well-known for throwing parties for her "A-list" celebrity friends, business partners, and fashionistas that made the pages of *Vogue Magazine.*

"Mrs. Reynolds, you are too kind," he replied placing his hand on his chest as if he had received the ultimate compliment. "I wanted to complete this wedding for Dixie. I know she is looking down on us and I want her to be pleased with the event."

"I meant what I said," she continued. "I think you need to go into business for yourself. You have the contacts, you have the experience, you have the respect of your team and you have 'the eye.' That's something they can't teach you. I would like to talk with you about working out a contract to be my event planner," she concluded.

"Are you serious? I would be honored! You know I have always loved doing your events," he said almost speechless. "Yes, yes, I will do it!"

"Then it's settled. I have contacts in Hollywood and I will be happy to help spread the word that an event by Marcus is sure to be unforgettable! If you need help finding a space, getting your business cards, letter head, anything . . . you just let me know. We'll work something out," she nodded and moved towards her next project.

"She is an absolute angel!" he said shaking his head as if to clear it. "I can't believe how generous she is. I love her, Georgia! I just love her!"

Cassandra Reynolds had demonstrated once again that when you had her support, she wholeheartedly gave it. She would help Marcus get his business started and make sure the "pixies" kept their jobs.

"Has everyone eaten yet?" Sarah called out over her radio. "If you haven't, come take a break while the cheese steaks are still hot!"

The "pixies" began heading toward the buffet table that had been set up and began helping themselves to sandwiches, homemade kettle chips, dill pickles and Sarah's Greek pasta salad, a tea room favorite. The tri-colored pasta was combined with Kalamata olives, sweet red onions, green peppers, chunks of feta cheese, and cherry tomatoes with a homemade Greek dressing.

"Don't forget to grab a slice of lemonade cake," she reminded everyone as they moved through the line.

"My favorite!" Shane grinned as he helped himself to a slice. The tart cake was layered with a sweet lemon glaze made from concentrated lemonade and confectioner's sugar. A coconut whipped cream frosting topped the yummy dessert.

"Thank you Sarah for doing this," I said acknowledging all her hard work on preparing our meal.

"It was my contribution. That and the sunflower kissing balls Tom and I worked on together. I think they are going to look so cute. Don't you?" she asked as giddy as a teenager just asked to her senior prom. She looked adorable with her ruffled pink and brown polka dot apron over her work clothes.

"I think the kissing balls are a nice touch. Olivia will love them," I said as I moved through the line and took my seat next to Shane.

"Did someone radio Carl to come join us?" Sarah asked Cassandra.

"Dan said he was working on the carriage up at the barn. He should come eat. Maybe he's about done," Cassandra thought out loud. "Carl, Carl, this is Cassandra. Do you read me?" she called into her receiver. There was static and a long pause. "Carl, do you read me?" she tried again. "That's strange. Maybe the barn doesn't get reception."

"I spoke with Carl just a few moments ago. He was getting ready to head down. Let me try," Dan said attempting to radio Carl. "He must be on his way. He'll be here shortly," he rationalized.

Matt Lincoln made a sudden appearance at the tent entrance. "What is going on in here?" he said looking surprised and pleased. "I guess it's safe to assume the wedding is still on for tomorrow?" he said hugging his mom and dad.

"What are you doing here? You're ruining your surprise!" Audrey chastised her towering son. "I thought you said you would be at the precinct all night."

"Actually, that's why I'm here. I'm following up on a lead and need to speak to Marcus," Lincoln answered.

"Have some dinner while you talk with him," Sarah offered him a plate. "Sit down and rest. After all, you have a very important day tomorrow."

"Thanks, Sarah. This looks delicious, much better than vending machine food. Where is my bride, by the way?" he said looking around the gathering of friends and family.

"At the farmhouse fast asleep," I answered. "Ruby and Laurel are with her and she does not suspect what's going on down here, so don't give it away!" I warned him.

"How did you get all this past her?" he said amazed.

"A glass of champagne, a Swedish massage and a spa-tini and your bride was wiped out!" Audrey teased. "She slept the whole ride back, poor thing. She was worn out and I imagine you are too," she said worried.

"I'm doing fine. Just closing in on our mystery business partner," he informed us. "That's why I need to speak with Marcus. He may know who she is."

"She? Dixie's business partner was a woman?" Cassandra sounded a bit perplexed. "I don't know why I assumed it was a man."

"Marcus, we found some contracts with the name Samantha August on them. Does that ring any bells to you?" Lincoln said sitting down next to Marcus.

"Hmm. Let me think. No, I don't remember a client or meeting a contact with that name. Do you Georgia?" he turned and asked the ponytailed "pixie."

"I don't know a Samantha August. Nope. Never heard of that person," she replied, "and I handled all of Dixie's correspondence when she had her surgeries."

"We are waiting for some surveillance video from the bank," Lincoln testified. "Apparently Dixie and this Samantha August had some business papers notarized at Dixie's bank in Hollywood. They have to make copies of driver's licenses when they notarize papers plus we are having them review their video from that date to see who this mystery woman is. The station will call me when they get it from California. I thought you might be able to take a look at it and tell me if you recognize her."

"Sure. I'll be happy to do it. Like I said, I don't know

anyone by that name. Do you Adam?"

"Sorry dude, I'm not good with names, remember?" Adam admitted.

"Does anyone know a Samantha August?" Lincoln asked the group.

"Wait! Sam is short for Samantha, right?" Adam said in shock. "Where is she anyway?"

"She was right next to me in line about ten minutes ago," Georgia testified. "I saw her right before Mr. Lincoln walked into the tent."

"And started talking about Dixie's business partner and surveillance video," Marcus said putting it together. "I think we know who Samantha August is and she's been right under our noses this entire time. I feel so violated!" Marcus moaned.

"Quick, call up to the house," Lincoln yelled at Cassandra. "We've got a suspect loose on the grounds. I'll call the station!"

"Dan, Dan, this is Carl," a low voice called over the radio.

"Come in Carl," Dan radioed back.

"We've got trouble. That woman with short black hair came into the barn and hit me in the head with a shovel. When I came to, Maggie May's stall door was open and the horse was gone. I think that woman took her," Carl groaned.

"Don't move, Carl. You may have a concussion. I'll send for an ambulance," Dan radioed back. "We've got a situation, Matt. She's on horseback. She could be anywhere in these mountains by now," Dan related to the police detective.

"I'll call for the search helicopter. You got an extra horse I can ride? I doubt she could be more than a few minutes ahead of us. You know these woods and land better than anyone. We have an advantage," he told the ranch foreman.

"Come on Bill," Dan urged his ranch hand. "Let's saddle up the horses and go after her."

"I'll go with you," Shane volunteered.

"Count me in, bro!" Tom called out. "We need all the manpower we can get."

"Let's ride, then!" Lincoln commanded.

"I'll call 911 and get an ambulance out here for Carl," Cassandra volunteered.

"You radio us if you see any sign of Sam or Samantha or whoever she is, all right?" Lincoln barked out at our group. "I am not letting her get away!"

TWENTY

"Have you heard anything yet?" I asked Detective Mansfield. He had set up a perimeter around the ranch and was coordinating the search. A makeshift headquarters had been set up adjacent to the tent.

"I've got deputies blocking off the major intersections coming off this mountain. She's not going to get very far. Don't you worry, Mrs. Spencer."

I was worried. Worried that Shane was riding in the dark after a woman that had killed two people and assaulted Carl. He was lucky. The emergency room doctor said if the blow to his head had been over one more inch, he would most likely have died from the attack. He was resting comfortably in a private room for overnight observation with a very worried Sheila at his side.

"So this Sam and Samantha August are definitely one in the same?" I asked still in shock. "We spent quite a bit of time with her this week. It really concerns me that she blended in so well without being detected." I thought back to all the concern she had given the other "pixies" when they learned of Austin's death at the Dogwood Inn. She was a chameleon, alright.

"When Matt called me with the update, I immediately dispatched two of my guys over to the inn. We found Trixie in Ms. August's room as well as Dixie's day planner. We've also had the LA police send her driver's license photo. Does this look like this Sam woman?" he asked showing it to me.

I studied the black and white photo. The face was the same, but the hair was much longer and more feminine. I had worked side by side all week with an imposter. It made my stomach turn just looking at the picture.

"Yes, that's her. I still can't believe she fooled all of us. Why would her silent business partner be working for her? That I don't understand," I commented to the detective.

"Maybe she wanted to keep a close eye on her investment. If what the bank records are showing about Dixie's spending habits are true, this Samantha August woman was probably concerned that her capital was being mismanaged," he surmised.

"Yes, and she had an addiction to plastic surgery from what her employees told us. That can be quite expensive," I stated.

"And a severe gambling habit. She had been to Vegas more than three times in the past two months. She spent money on posh hotel rooms, theatre tickets, expensive dinners and high stakes poker games. She had a standing reservation at the Wynn Hotel for the presidential suite," he confided.

"Wow. She was living the big life. It will eventually catch up with you!" I warned.

"And unfortunately for her it did. People get angry and do crazy things when you fool with their money," he said matter-of-factly.

"Have you heard anything yet?" Cassandra asked worried for the umpteenth time.

"Not yet, Mrs. Reynolds but you'll be one of the first to know. If you'll excuse me."

"I hope they catch her! I can't believe she was with us all week. It really makes me uncomfortable that we were rubbing elbows with Dixie and Austin's killer. And we had no clue!" she said rather tormented.

"How could we have known, Cassandra? She is a pro. Detective Mansfield was just telling me about Dixie's gambling debts and trips to Vegas. Who do we really know anyway? You had no idea that Dixie had a gambling addiction," I reminded her.

"And the affair with Austin, the plastic surgery, not paying her vendors. I am very upset about all of this right now. I hope they catch this Sam woman and lock her up for good!" she shouted.

"We just got a call from Lincoln," Mansfield said running back towards us. "The perp rode her horse into the river and was apparently thrown off. We've got men headed downstream to see if they can find her."

"Downstream where?" Cassandra inquired.

"About three miles above the Old Mill. If she goes over that waterfall, she's as good as dead," Mansfield remarked.

"Come on, Amelia! We can drive down and see what happens," Cassandra whispered loudly in my ear. "I want to see her get caught. I've got to make sure that Dixie didn't die in vain."

"I want to see her caught as much as you do, but I don't think it's a good idea. We'll just be in the way," I argued.

"I'm going. You can stay here if you choose, but I'm going to be there, come hell or high water!" she shouted.

We jumped in my VW bug. I shot past the front entrance as fast as I felt comfortable driving the winding country roads at night. It was pitch black and growing foggier. I had to slam on my breaks as we approached an officer at a road block, flares lit and blue police lights flashing.

"Oh great, now what?" Cassandra moaned.

"Hello officer. We've got to get down the mountain," I told the uniformed man as I rolled the window down.

"I need to see some ID please," he gruffly stated. Both Cassandra and I opened our wallets and removed our driver's licenses and handed them to the solemn policeman.

"Thank you," he said returning them to us and shining his flashlight around the back seat of the car. "You won't be going this way. We've got the road blocked and no one is getting through. We have an active man hunt going on."

"We need to get to the Old Mill right away. Can't you let us through?" Cassandra pleaded.

"No, I'm under strict orders. But you can turn around and take the shortcut just past the turn off and it will take you over to the mill. We use that back road all the time. Be careful, it's a bit washed out in places after last year's rock slide," he warned us.

"Thank you, sir," I said putting "lady bug" in reverse and turning around.

"I know where the pass is up here on the left," Cassandra said helping me to navigate. "Here! Here! Turn!" she yelled as I almost drove past it in the thick fog.

I cut sharply to the left and skidded onto the two lane winding road. It was rough and had many pot holes. I carefully maneuvered around them to the best of my ability and held on to my steering wheel tightly. The road was indeed washed out in some spots and I teetered close to the edge as I kept my eyes firmly glued on the road in front of me.

"I hope no one else is headed this way," I said nervously. "I don't think there's enough good road to pass someone."

"Gun it, Amelia!" Cassandra screeched. "No one is driving out here tonight. We've got to make sure they catch this Samantha woman so I can see Dixie's killer caught!"

"I'm going as fast as I can. I don't know what you want me to do? I'm just hoping we don't go over the edge of the mountain!" I panicked. "The police will make sure they catch her. She's in the river. There's no way she's getting away."

"She could pull herself out and escape in the woods," Cassandra continued.

"You think she's in top shape? That's a pretty swift current. I don't think she's going to be able to fight it and get to the riverbank without assistance," I said.

"Have you seen *The Fugitive?* People can climb out of swiftly moving rivers. I'm not taking a chance of letting her get away!" Cassandra said confidently.

"We're almost there," I announced as we came down to the bottom of the last curve. "The Old Mill is down here on the right." I drove the last five hundred yards and pulled in front of the two-hundred-year-old building that still provided freshly ground cornmeal to the residents of Dogwood Cove. It had withstood fires and the occasional tornado to remain one of our town's oldest landmarks.

"Have you got a flashlight in your glove box?" she asked flipping the small compartment open.

"I've got one in the trunk," I said as I rapidly moved to

the rear of the car and opened the trunk searching for the emergency box Shane had put together for me.

"What's in this? *MacGyver's* long lost box of tricks?" Cassandra teased as she pushed aside jumper cables, tire flat, and matches. "Hey, are these flares?"

"Yeah, Shane always thought it was best to be prepared for any emergency."

"We could light these suckers and help illuminate the riverbank," she said quite pleased with her resourcefulness.

"Do you think we should?" I questioned.

"I don't see any police support down here yet or the search helicopter. This could help mark the area just before the waterfall," she hoped.

"If she hasn't already gone over and that's a big if judging by how the river is running tonight," I said looking at the bank.

"Let's do it!" Cassandra said reaching for the matches. I grabbed the flashlight and flares and shut the trunk. We both moved at lightning speed to the river bank, my flashlight beam leading the way.

"Here, give me those!" Cassandra yelled excitedly. "Whoa!" she said as she lit the first flare and held it as far away from her as she could. "Wow, they are blindingly!" she screamed as she laid the first flare on the ground. "Quick, give me the next one!"

I handed her the flares one-by-one until all four were lit. It did brighten the area and almost looked like daylight.

"Now what?" I asked as we looked around.

"We wait," she said loudly looking intently at the rushing current.

"Cassandra, Amelia, can you hear me?" Sarah could be heard in our earbuds. I had forgotten we still had those on.

"I hear you Sarah! Over!" I yelled above the sound of rushing water.

"Where are you? Detective Mansfield was looking for you," she reported.

"We're down by the Old Mill," Cassandra yelled.

"The Old Mill? What the dickens?" Sarah said bewildered.

"We have flares lit to help find Sam," I told her.

"I don't think Detective Mansfield will be too happy to hear this," Sarah warned.

"So don't tell him where we are," Cassandra said rather acerbically.

"From what he's telling me, this Samantha woman may have a gun on her. She is registered as owning a derringer."

"Great! She may have a gun, Cassandra. What are we going to do if she crawls up the riverbank with a gun?" I asked nervously.

"*If* and that's a big if, she has a gun, it's a wet gun by now. I doubt it would still fire," she stated sounding quite reasonable.

"I think guns still fire when they are wet. Maybe if it had been underwater and corroded it wouldn't work, but I'm willing to bet it would still fire if the powder isn't wet in the shell casing."

"Come back to the ranch! You don't want to run into a crazy woman being chased as a suspect in a double murder!" Sarah begged over the radio.

"She's right, Cassandra. What in the world are we doing out here?" I said looking about nervously. "This Sammantha woman is a fruit cake and has murdered two people. I'd like to stay as far away from her as possible," I rationalized.

"This is Sarah, the same Sarah who risked her life to save your Aunt Imogene before she became the next victim of the Andrew Johnson Bridge murderer. She obviously didn't follow her own advice during that investigation, did she?" Cassandra systematically beat down Sarah's influence.

"Yes, the same Sarah who researches the paranormal. But she's right, Cassandra. This is dangerous!" I argued.

"We've come this far. What if she floats right by here? Are we going to let her get away?" she debated.

"And if she does float by, what do you think we should do? Jump in and go over the falls with her? That's over a two hundred foot drop. There's no way I'm getting into that frigid water and ending up dead from hypothermia!" I concluded.

The night air was getting increasingly damp and chilly and I felt myself shiver involuntarily. I wasn't sure if it was the drop in temperature or the thought of dealing with a mad woman. My instincts were telling me to get the heck out of there and hurry!

"The police haven't even made it here yet. We could be providing much needed help in watching the river and keeping the banks lit for them. We can't leave now!" she said emphatically. "You can go but I'm staying!"

"And I thought Olivia was the stubborn one. Cassandra, I'm not leaving you out here by yourself. We either both stay or we both leave," I said determined not to leave my friend alone in a dangerous situation.

"Should have left when you had the chance," a wet and angry Sam said coming out of the shadows of the Old Mill structure. Her black pants and turtleneck were clinging to her wet form. She was pointing a small gun directly at us.

"Ms. August, I presume!" Cassandra said snidely not daring to show any sign of nervousness. "We are now officially introduced. I hope your river experience wasn't too cold. It looks like you are freezing," she taunted as she watched the rail thin Samantha's teeth chatter. "If you don't get some dry clothes on, you'll die from exposure and we can't have that, can we?"

"I meant to thank you for making it so easy to see my way to the bank of the river," Samantha returned the sarcastic remark. "These flares turned out to be very helpful!" she said as she continued to shake in the cold air. "You're right. I do need to change into some dry clothes and yours will do just fine, Mrs. Reynolds," she said pointing her derringer at Cassandra's midriff. "I believe we're about the same size."

"You've got to be kidding. I'm not giving you my clothes," Cassandra said defiantly.

"Take them off and throw them over here," Samantha motioned with her gun. "I said now!" she screamed cocking the hammer of the gun.

"You better listen to her, Cassandra!" I persuaded my dear companion. "Please do what she says!"

"At least one of you has sense. Do what she says and no one will get hurt!" Samantha August yelled.

"Is that what you told Dixie? Do what I say and no one will get hurt before you hit her in the head like a coward and dragged her into Jack's stall?" Cassandra taunted.

"Quit running your mouth and take off your clothes!" Samantha hissed.

"No problem," Cassandra said removing her wool coat and throwing it next to the angry woman. "I just thought you could help me understand why you had to kill Dixie. What did she ever do to you to deserve to die?" she asked as she unbuttoned her pants and slid them down to her ankles.

"She spent my money on herself and her little gigolo Austin. She tricked me. She got me to invest my entire savings into her business and then blew it on her gambling, her plastic surgery and her extravagant spending. I watched every penny I earned go up in smoke!" she screeched.

"I can understand why you are upset, believe me. I'm upset with her too. But murder? Why kill her? You'll never get your investment back now!" Cassandra logically said.

"I gave her every chance in the world to change, to get her bad habits under control. Why do you think I was working with her? I needed to keep an eye on my investment and make sure she wasn't blowing any more of my money. She owed me almost seven hundred thousand dollars!" she said and began crying. The gun shook in her left hand as she wiped her nose with the back of her right arm and continued to point the gun at us.

"And no one knew who you were? Not even Marcus?" I asked dumbfounded.

"I was a new hire. That's all they knew. I made Dixie agree to let me join the team anonymously. That was my final condition or I was going to sue her for breach of contract," she informed us as Cassandra slowly kept removing layers of clothing. "Hurry up and quit stalling!"

"But why kill her? What could you possibly gain from her death?" Cassandra continued the interrogation.

"I've got about a million reasons why as in a million dollars," she bragged. She owed me what was rightfully mine and my life insurance policy on our business partnership guaranteed I would get my money back!"

"What about Austin? Why kill him? What did he ever do to you?" Cassandra asked as she stood in her boots and undergarments shivering in the cold.

"Don't you get it? Austin was all part of the plan from the beginning," Samantha said as she carefully took off her turtleneck never taking her eyes from us. "Austin and I were involved. I got him the job with Dixie to keep an eye on her."

"Well that must have really irritated you when he began taking trips with her and spending your money," Cassandra goaded. "Did you know he and Dixie had become lovers or was that part of the plan too?"

"He never cared about her. He used her to get information for me. You think that old goat would appeal to someone as young as Austin?" she sneered as she began slipping on the dry pants.

"So why kill him? Did you catch him in the hen house with someone else?" Cassandra provoked the diabolical killer. I couldn't imagine why Cassandra was so intent on questioning her. I personally didn't want to further upset such an unstable individual.

"It was really quite simple. I couldn't afford to have any witnesses. Austin was collateral damage," she smiled as she slipped Cassandra's wool coat over her dry clothes. "I'm going to need the boots too."

"Here, take them!" Cassandra yelled as she threw one at a time in Samantha's direction.

"So you told him to meet you for a little lover's rendezvous in Dixie's room? What is that all about? Some sick kind of joke?"

"Austin was quite impressive in bed. I thought we could have one more romp before I had to get rid of him," she boasted. "I couldn't let Dixie have all the fun with him!"

"You are really twisted, aren't you? How pathetic you are!"

"Cassandra hush!" I implored my outspoken friend. I felt as though she were pushing Samantha to the very edge of her sanity.

"Pathetic am I? I've watched you for a long time, Mrs. Reynolds. You have no idea what pathetic truly is. You're the one who has been played by Dixie!" she retorted.

"Played by Dixie? What are you talking about?" Cassandra said straightening her back to stand at her full height. I took off my jacket and handed it to her so at least she could stay partially warm.

"Dixie and that husband of yours," she laughed as she watched the realization dawn on Cassandra's face. "Didn't you know? Oh please! All those campaign fundraising parties and the inaugural ball. You didn't have any idea of what was going on right under your nose. You're the pathetic one!" she crowed.

Oh my heavens! Doug Reynolds had not been having an affair with his campaign manager Penelope. It was actually Dixie Beauregard. Oh I felt my stomach lurch as I looked over and saw the hurt on Cassandra's face. She had suspected as much, but just had mistrusted the wrong woman.

"Hand me the keys!" Samantha barked at me. "Hurry up!" she screamed.

"Here take them," I said throwing them above her head

and beyond her reach. She lunged in the air to try to catch them and turned to look on the ground to see where they had landed.

"Cute one! You'll pay for that," she threatened as she turned to pick them up. Just then Cassandra moved to the left and quickly grabbed one of the lit flares. She ran towards Samantha and rammed it into her back. I watched horrified as the coat she was wearing began to catch fire. She screamed out in pain and dropped to the ground and rolled to put out the flame.

"Stop right there!" Detective Mansfield yelled rushing towards the injured woman. "You are under arrest for the murders of Dixie Beauregard and Austin Foster," he announced as he easily turned her onto her stomach and cuffed her hands behind her back.

"I am so glad to see you!" I admitted.

"Thank your friend Ms. McCaffrey. She told me where you were and I decided to head over here. Looks like I got here just in time!"

"What happened?" Sarah asked rushing up to hug both of us. "Where are your clothes, Cassandra?"

"It's a long story. Let's get out of here before I hurt her some more," she advised us.

"I have a blanket in the car," I remembered as I walked over to where I had chucked my keys. "You are going to be in prison for a long time! Enjoy your stay! Guess you won't be collecting that money now," I informed the now subdued Samantha August. "She had a million dollar life insurance policy on Dixie and was involved with Austin. There's your motive!" I said as I walked by Detective Mansfield.

"I'll need you and Mrs. Reynolds to come by the station and give a statement," he told me.

"We'll be right there after I get some warm clothes for Cassandra," I told him retrieving my keys. "Come on Cassandra and Sarah! Let's get out of here," I said turning away from the Old Mill. I hoped we would all rest easier now that Dixie's killer had been caught. Unfortunately for Cassandra, her nightmare was just beginning.

TWENTY ONE

"What do you think she will do?" Shane asked me as we lay in bed discussing the night's events. I couldn't sleep. I was too keyed up from our confrontation with Samantha and the terror of having a gun pointed at me.

"I don't know. I didn't dare bring it up since Doug drove her to the police station. She asked me to take her home so she could get some warm clothes and told me she would meet me later. I was shocked to see her walk in with Doug," I confided to my husband.

"Do you think they will work things out? I don't condone his behavior, but they have been married almost twenty years. I'd hate to see their marriage break up over an indiscretion."

"Cassandra has shared with me that she and Doug have been having problems since his campaign began. She's been going to counseling . . . alone. I don't know what she will end up doing, but the puzzle pieces are falling in place. Dixie was a large part of Doug's campaign and she was around quite a bit last year. I think Cassandra feels betrayed by both of them," I concluded intertwining my fingers with Shane's. Thank goodness we had not had to face such an obstacle in our marriage. I couldn't imagine the hurt Cassandra was feeling right now.

"Maybe it was a lie and this Samantha woman was lashing out at Cassandra. Could that be a possibility?" he asked hopefully.

I snuggled deeper under the covers, my body slowly warming and relaxing. I began to yawn before I answered Shane.

"Cassandra wouldn't be going to counseling if everything was fine between the two of them. Shane, he won't even go with her. I don't know what to think of him anymore. I didn't even know how to act towards him at the station. It has put me in a very uncomfortable position because Cassandra is my dear friend," I told my sweet husband.

"I'm glad you and Cassandra didn't get hurt. I can't imagine my life without you in it!" he said lovingly looking at me. "Promise me that you won't go off on some half-cocked adventure again!"

"It wasn't my idea. I wanted to turn around and leave and then there she was!" I said defensively.

"You are a mother of two, a wife and a business owner. You shouldn't risk your life by chasing after a murder suspect," he reminded me.

"And you were on horseback riding in the dark through the mountains looking for the same murder suspect. Isn't that the pot calling the kettle black?" I teased.

"But I had Lincoln with me and he was packing heat," he smiled and rubbed my arm. "Are you getting warm yet?"

"Yes and sleepy. We were packing our own heat called a flare. Who would have thought a flare could be used as a weapon?"

"Quick thinking on Cassandra's part. I would have loved to see her standing there in her underwear attacking

Samantha with a lit flare," he laughed. "That woman has some hutzpah!"

"It wasn't funny, Shane Spencer!" I said smacking his arm playfully. "She was freezing to death. I think when Samantha told her about Doug and Dixie, she snapped and that woman had no idea the wrath she unleashed upon herself. It was akin to a primal instinct!"

"It was a survival instinct. Cassandra knew that Samantha could shoot both of you after she took the car keys and be long gone before anyone found you. She just didn't count on the 'warrior princess' attacking her," he snickered and pulled the duvet cover closer around my neck. "You get some sleep. Tomorrow is a big day!"

"Don't remind me! I still have a million things to do in the morning," I moaned and shut my eyes tightly.

"And they will wait until the morning. I'll help you so we will get the list done in half the time," he reassured me and turned off the light.

"I love you Shane Spencer. I'm so glad you are mine!"

"So am I. Love you sweetheart. Sweet dreams!"

I hoped I could sleep. Tomorrow would be a very busy day. The wedding!

TWENTY-TWO

"*I* feel like you are scalping me, Armando!" Olivia winced as the hairdresser teased her hair and sprayed another coat of hairspray.

"Do you want to look gorgeous today or not? I can put my comb down and walk away right now or we can finish and make you a beautiful bride," he playfully teased Olivia. "No pain, no gain right ladies!"

"Just hurry up and get it over with and stop shellacking me with that hideous hair spray!" she complained.

"You take my breath away, Liv!" Ruby told her only child as she kissed her on forehead. "Here, have a mimosa. It will help you relax."

"I don't need any help relaxing. I'm fine. Isn't that right, Amelia?"

"You're doing great, Liv! Just let Armando work his magic," I encouraged the very nervous bride. She took small sips of her champagne cocktail and attempted to enjoy herself.

"Where's Cassandra? Has anyone seen her this morning?" she excitedly looked around the salon.

"She's picking up a few last minute things. She called and she will be here soon," Sarah reassured her. She had already had her hair finished by one of Armando's team members and was in the process of having her makeup professionally applied.

"I hope she isn't going to be much longer. I don't need my matron-of-honor holding up the wedding," Olivia grumbled.

"Cassandra is tying up some loose ends. She'll be here. Focus, Olivia, focus!" I encouraged her.

"Is it hot in here or is it just me?" she asked fanning herself.

"I think our little bride has a case of the jitters," Armando laughed and looked around the salon for confirmation.

"I do not have the jitters. I'm as calm as a cucumber," Olivia stated and put her hand flat in front of her to demonstrate her state of mind.

"Everyone gets a little nervous on their wedding day. You wouldn't be normal if you didn't get butterflies," Grandmother Laurel said coming to the rescue of her granddaughter. "I remember the day I married your grandfather. He was such a handsome man. I remember looking down the aisle and seeing him waiting for me. It's so vivid just like it happened yesterday," she said as a warm smiled spread across her face. "And I remember your father on his wedding day. Such a handsome man! I miss them both so much!"

"Oh Grandma! Please don't get me crying," Olivia pleaded as her eyes misted. "I will ruin my makeup and Jane will have to start all over again," she said fanning her eyes to stop watering. "I should have eloped! This is crazy!"

"You love the attention and you know it," Cassandra said waltzing into Armando's salon. "I stopped by the Dogwood Bakery and picked up some breakfast for all of us. I bet you haven't eaten anything. Have you?" she asked Olivia.

"No. I don't feel like I can hold anything down. My stomach is burning!" she admitted.

"You better eat something so you don't pass out during the ceremony. Here, have a chocolate croissant. I'm sure you could use some caffeine. I should have picked up some coffee."

"Amelia brought hot tea for all of us. She made a blend just for today in honor of the wedding. What did you call it again?" Olivia turned her head to ask me.

I named it 'Wedding Bells' in honor of today. It's a blend of rose petals, cherries and green sencha. It's great hot or iced. It's simply divine," I said pouring Cassandra a tea cup full.

"Oh it smells heavenly," she said closing her eyes and inhaling the sweet aromas. "I can really smell the cherry. This should be a great pick-me-up this morning."

"How are you?" I quietly asked her as I watched her take a sip.

"I'm doing fine, all things considered. Olivia doesn't know anything about last night, does she?" she whispered to me.

"Not a thing. Lincoln is going to wait until after the wedding to fill her in on Samantha. He doesn't want anything to ruin today. Doesn't she look beautiful?" I said turning to look at Olivia again as Armando expertly smoothed her hair and spun her around for us to admire. He had placed a headband of rhinestone encrusted dragon flies in her hair. The effect was stunning.

"She certainly does," Cassandra said setting down her tea cup and grabbing both of Olivia's hands. "I can't believe today is finally here. Liv, I'm so very happy for you!" Cassandra beamed a smile of sheer delight at her best friend. "I do have some news to tell you. Doug was called back to Nashville this morning. He sends his regrets," Cassandra informed her.

"Oh dear! Who will give me away, then?" Olivia said in alarm.

"If it's alright with you, Lewis would like the honor of giving you away," Audrey Lincoln spoke up. "We discussed it last night and I think it would be fitting since we already consider you our daughter," she said hugging Olivia.

"That's a terrific idea," Cassandra agreed turning away from the scene and wiping tears from her eyes.

"Hang in there," I said softly and handed her a tissue.

"I want to focus on Olivia and enjoy today. It isn't every day that your best friend gets married. I'm so happy for both of them. Lincoln is good for her and they have my blessing," she said beginning to cry openly.

"What's wrong, Cassandra? You cry at the drop of a hat!" Olivia joked.

"Oh you know me so well. I'm a sentimental fool when it comes to weddings. Just ignore me! Liv, I'm so happy for you both!" she said carefully kissing her on the cheek. "I don't want to mess up your makeup. Armando, you've done such a wonderful job! Look at her. She looks like a redhaired version of Anne Hathaway!"

"Anne Hathaway? Are you serious from *The Princess Diaries?* Is that before or after she had her eyebrows waxed and her hair tamed?" Olivia challenged Cassandra.

"After! After, of course!" Cassandra laughed. "Now eat up!" she commanded as we all enjoyed the camaraderie.

"Speaking of Lewis, he and the boys are at the General Morgan Inn getting ready. Anything you want me to tell

Matt when I speak to him?" Audrey asked her soon-to-be daughter-in-law.

"Tell him I love him and I can't wait to get married," Olivia spoke up.

"Tell him yourself!" Audrey Lincoln grinned as her handsome son strode into the salon carrying a dozen red long stemmed roses. The center of each rose was studded with a large crystal. They were absolutely beautiful.

"Lincoln! What are you doing here? It's bad luck to see the bride on the day of the wedding!" Sarah gasped from the makeup chair.

"Ever since I met you Olivia Rivers, I've had nothing but good luck," he said laying the bouquet in his bride's arms. "I remember the day you walked into the Dallas police department, all cocky and full of spirit. I knew then that I had met someone who would not only challenge me, but be my equal in every way," he said wiping the tears from Olivia's eyes.

"Oh my stars!" Cassandra whispered. "I love this man!" We all stood still watching the scene play out before us, witnesses to such a loving and touching moment.

"There hasn't been a dull moment since. And today, I would be honored if you would be my wife and share my life with me," he said tenderly kissing her. "And I would also be honored if you would wear this," he stated opening a black velvet jewelry box.

Olivia gasped as she looked at the necklace her groom took out and carefully fastened around her neck. She gazed into the mirror and touched the large tear drop shaped emerald surrounded by diamonds. I realized it matched her engagement ring as well as the earrings he had given her.

"Oh, Matt! It's stunning!" Olivia said giving him a long kiss. "You really know how to surprise a girl!"

"I don't want to keep you ladies from your appointments. Goodbye mother," he said and affectionately kissed her cheek. "Liv, I'll be waiting at the altar," he said as he exited the salon.

"You better snatch him up before I do," Armando told Olivia. "You are one lucky girl!"

"Yes she is," Ruby agreed. "Oh Olivia! What a beautiful necklace. He's a prince among men!"

"That he is, Ruby," Cassandra agreed. "That he is! Armando, let's get this lady to the church on time!"

TWENTY-THREE

Olivia descended carefully from the white carriage taking the hand of Lewis Lincoln for assistance. The toes of her red ostrich boots peeked from beneath the candlelit satin mermaid skirt, an accessory she insisted on wearing. Her hair was pulled back and held in place by her dragonfly headband. Auburn ringlets cascaded down her back and were covered with a simple tulle veil. The sweetheart neckline of her dress showcased her emerald necklace, which glinted in the bright sunlight. She had never looked more elegant.

She smiled as he tucked her hand in the crook of his arm and led her down the aisle. The pathway was formed by a carpet of autumn leaves in various shades of umber, gold and burnt cyana. A series of rustic trellises were staggered every six feet leading to the gazebo that Dan and the ranch hands had built alongside the pond. The Smoky Mountains made a majestic background and were reflected in the water's surface.

The ETSU bluegrass band plucked the traditional processional wedding Cannon in D as she slowly glided towards her groom. The mandolin, dulcimer, fiddle and guitar harmony brought together sounds reminiscent of a simpler time in our Appalachian community. It was as though she were being serenaded by past generations who had also shared this land.

As Olivia approached the first trellis, she was greeted by two of her riding students on either side. They presented her with clusters of sunflowers and small orange roses. She stopped to receive a hug from each of them and continued down the aisle to the next trellis and her next two students. A complete bouquet was fashioned by the time she greeted her groom at the ceremony site. It was a sweet touch to incorporate so many of the children who had benefitted from lessons under her guidance at the ranch. Many of the guests standing on each side of the pathway wiped their eyes as they watched the loving embraces the children exchanged with their teacher.

"She is gorgeous," Cassandra sighed as she stood next to me. She looked chic in a plum satin sheath dress. "I'm so happy for her today!" she said carefully dabbing her eyes and watching her best friend descend the aisle.

I smiled across to Shane who looked so handsome in his dark blue suit. He was standing next to a very happy Tom who was acting as best man. Matt Lincoln stood as if at attention, never taking his eyes off his beautiful bride. The loving way he watched Olivia approach the altar was not lost on anyone. His adoration was written all over his chiseled face.

I looked to my right at Sarah who was wearing a bridesmaid's dress in a deeper shade of burgundy with a plunging back. She had opted to wear contacts today instead of her signature red-rimmed glasses. I thought she looked a bit like a glamorous version of Tina Fey dressed for the Emmy awards. She too was beaming as she watched Olivia.

As the minister began the ceremony, I turned to the front row of seats and was tickled to see Audrey Lincoln seated next to Ruby Rivers, holding her hand. The two had opted to disregard the tradition of the mother-of-the-bride on one side of the aisle and the groom's mother on the other side. Instead they decided to sit together unified as one family giving their blessing to this couple. I was delighted to see how in just a few days' time, these two strong-willed matriarchs had formed such a tight bond. Laurel Rivers sat next to Ruby openly weeping.

The minister motioned for everyone to sit down. "Who gives this woman away?" his voiced boomed on this warm autumn day.

"Her mother, Ruby and I do," a confident Lewis Lincoln replied as he kissed Olivia sweetly on the cheek. "Welcome to our family," he said as he presented her hand to his son. The men shook hands and embraced. "Take good care of her, son!"

"I intend to do that for the rest of my life," Matt Lincoln told his father as he took Olivia's small hands in his. "You look stunning Olivia. You have made me the happiest man in the world today."

As the minister continued the ceremony, I gazed lovingly at my own husband and exchanged glances with him. I was thinking back to our wedding day and our vows. I felt an involuntary lump in my throat as my eyes burned with tears. I would forever be grateful for this wonderful man and the life and family we shared. I know he too was reminiscing about our nuptials as he acknowledged me from across the aisle. I looked out at Charlie and Emma sitting with Aunt Alice and sighed contentedly. Life was good.

"I now pronounce you husband and wife. You may kiss your bride and Olivia, you may kiss your groom!" the minister said jovially. I guess he had received the memo that our bride was independent and an equal opportunist!

Matt Lincoln leaned down to embrace his petite bride and leaned her back for an extended romantic kiss. He then gathered her up in his arms and carried her down the long aisle.

"What are you doing? You are crazy!" she laughed. "Matt, put me down!" she protested.

"I'm never letting you go, Liv! Not in a million years," he informed her as the crowd of over one hundred fifty guests stood up and cheered. Everyone was overjoyed at the union of this couple and knew in their hearts they had what it took to share a happy life together.

I took Shane's hand and squeezed it as we followed the recessional and joined the wedding guests in the nearby tent for cocktails. The front pasture had been erased of any trace of last night's makeshift police headquarters. The ETSU bluegrass band strolled alongside the guests and continued strumming their instruments and singing as they made their way to the reception. Servers presented guests with fall cocktails designed for the affair. They were made with a thyme infused simple syrup, apple cider and apple brandy garnished with a fresh slice of apple.

"Oh my goodness! Who did all this?" Olivia exclaimed as she entered the fabulous wedding venue. "Where was I when all this was being transformed?"

"Asleep in the farmhouse," Ruby Rivers informed her daughter. "Your friends put this all together yesterday."

"You're kidding me! I can't believe you did all this for me!"

she said hugging Sarah, Cassandra and myself in a group embrace. "Thank you!"

"Thank Marcus and his entourage," Cassandra told her. "They worked all night to pull this off and he did an outstanding job!"

"Where is Marcus?" Matt questioned. "I want to shake his hand. This looks exactly like what Olivia envisioned for our wedding. It's as if he read her mind."

"He's over there," I said waving at Marcus who was dressed in a black pinstripe suit standing at the edge of the tent. He was busy helping the musicians set up for the party. "Come here, Marcus!"

He quickly strode across the dance floor and kissed the bride's cheek. "I hope you are happy with everything," he said and leaned close to her.

"It's perfect. How did you get everything just right? From the pumpkin and ivy topiaries, to the table centerpieces, to the ceiling, just look at this! I can never thank you enough!" she said as she hugged him.

"I'm so glad you're pleased. It was my pleasure!" he answered. "Come here and look at your place settings," he said as he led her to the head table. Low center pieces of sunflowers mixed with deep orange roses and red pepper berries designed by Herb from Floral Fantasies were accented by flickering candles in various heights running down the length of the tables. The pillar candles were embellished with maple and oak leaves wrapped around them and finished with raffia.

"Look at these plates! They are gorgeous," Olivia gushed lifting the burgundy pastoral toile pattern and admiring them. "Where in the world did you find these?"

"Oh, I have my connections," Marcus grinned pleased with himself. "I knew you would love them."

"You thought of everything I wanted. How did you know?" Olivia said excitedly.

"I listened to your vision for your wedding back in the planning stages. I try to take my brides theme and blow the roof off!" he said waving his hands around.

"He listened to you," Cassandra told her. "He's good at what he does. This is just spectacular," she complimented Marcus. "I look forward to working with you on future projects."

"Future projects? Is something going on between you two?" Olivia inquired.

"A wonderful business partnership," Marcus confided. "I better get back to work and make sure the food is ready," he said taking his exit.

"This has been the most perfect day," Olivia said as she looked around the tent at her friends and family. "I can't believe everyone worked so hard to make today happen. I'm just overwhelmed right now," she said beginning to cry.

"Don't you dare mess up your makeup!" Armando fussed as he approached our small group. "I'm here if you need touch ups," he told her as he moved to a nearby table.

"Everyone is here. It feels like the entire community turned out for this," Olivia smiled as she cast a glance around the tent.

She was right. There was John Gambino proudly standing next to his ice sculpture depicting Olivia's prized mare, Maggie May. He was dressed in a chef's coat and was assisting Edna of Elegant Edibles in attending the impressive buffet that was set up on the far side of the tent. Margaret

Dunn and Wanda Given from the Dogwood Inn waved from across the room enjoying the day's festivities.

It looked as though the entire Dogwood Cove police department was in attendance with their spouses. I also noticed Dan and Bill with their wives finding a seat next to Carl and Sheila. I hoped those two had resolved their issues and Carl had learned his lesson. He had a small bandage on his head, a reminder of his run in with Samantha August the previous evening.

Aunt Imogene decked out in a Cheetah print suit had already found her way to the dance floor with a distinguished looking gentleman. They were dancing to the Tennessee Waltz as a young bluegrass performer sang her sweet rendition backed up with a fiddle and mandolin. Imogene blew me a quick kiss as her date spun her around the floor.

"Who is that with Aunt Imogene?" I asked Lucy Lyle who had walked over to greet me.

"Oh that's our neighbor, Kent Simpson. He's new to the area. He moved down the street a few weeks ago. Imogene decided to be his personal tour guide of Dogwood Cove," Lucy stated in a flat voice.

"Should I start planning another wedding?" I teased.

"I think five is enough. She's just having fun," Lucy reassured me. "You look beautiful Amelia. That color suits you!"

"Thanks Lucy! I love it too. Olivia picked out our dresses."

"She's really come a long way," Lucy commented. "I never thought I'd see that girl in a dress let alone a fancy reception like this," she said as she watched Olivia and Lincoln waltz around the dance floor. "He's really brought the best out in her."

And he had. I thought back to Olivia just two years ago before she had met Matt Lincoln. She was alone, fiercely independent, brazen and razor tongued. Cassandra had slowly been transforming our little cowgirl into her inner Santa Fe diva, but it had taken time. The change in her personality had occurred when she began dating Lincoln and had started to build a relationship with trust at its core. To look at her today, it would be hard to believe she was the same high-spirited woman who had strode into the Dallas police precinct ready to rumble with anyone who crossed her path.

"You're off in another world. What were you thinking about?" Shane asked as he led me to the dance floor.

"I was thinking about how much everyone has changed," I told him as we moved to the music.

"Changed how?" he said placing his head closer to mine.

"Well look at Olivia. She's never been happier and now she's married. I never thought she was the marrying type."

"Aha," he said in agreement.

And Sarah, she's a business owner now. She's grown and stretched in so many ways since she left the library and took over the Pink Dogwood Tea Room."

"You miss the business, don't you?" he said knowingly.

"Sure I miss it, but I'm happy with Smoky Mountain Coffee, Herb and Tea Company. I miss the day to day running of the tea room, but I enjoy what we're doing," I told him.

"So what's wrong?" he said pulling back a bit to look at my face. "Something's bothering you."

"And then there's Cassandra. . ."

"She'll land on her feet Amelia. She's a strong woman," he reassured me.

"I wonder what will happen next. What changes are in store next for all of us?"

We stopped dancing as Marcus announced the cutting of the cake. I joined all the other friends and family as we gathered around the towering confectionary masterpiece and watched our dear friends begin their lives together symbolized by the cutting of the cake. I watched as the two love birds entwined their arms and fed each other.

"Today was perfect Shane. I hope we have more special days like this," I said as my eyes misted with tears. The Traveling Tea Ladies had been on many adventures together. Though our lives were taking very different paths, one thing remained constant. We would always be close friends and we would always be there for each other through the ups and downs.

TWENTY-FOUR

"And that's when a coyote walked right in front of our mule and nearly spooked him," Olivia related to our small gathering as we hung on her every word. Lincoln had his arm around his new bride and happiness radiated from every single pore of his being.

"I've always wanted to go the Grand Canyon. It's on my bucket list," Sarah revealed to us. "I would like to go to one of those Indian sweat tents and be one with nature just like *Dances With Wolves*," she sighed and looked off into the distance.

"You had me up until sweat tent," Olivia laughed. "The last thing I want to do is have a hallucination out in the middle of the desert, far away from an emergency room, sitting naked with strangers in a sweat tent. Where do you come up with these ideas? People have died in those things."

"I think it sounds like a fun trip," Cassandra declared. "I for one am ready for something adventurous," she said sounding a bit hollow.

I exchanged knowing glances with Shane as he patted my leg under the table in reaffirmation. Cassandra was hosting the dinner celebration tonight at her lakeside home and was doing her best to attend to her hostess duties. I knew she was under a terrible strain, but she had privately told me she was determined not to let her marital problems interfere with welcoming the newlyweds home. The dinner party in her lavishly decorated dining room would serve as a distraction from her struggles with Doug.

"Who would care for some more champagne?" she recited as she moved around the table refilling glasses.

"Thank you Cassandra," Matt Lincoln said as he moved his flute to make pouring easier. "This was just delicious. I cannot think of the last time I enjoyed lamb more than tonight. Everything was perfect!"

"It was my pleasure," she said as she continued pouring champagne for our small group. "Actually, thank the chef. If I had prepared the lamb, we would be calling the fire department."

"How is everything going with your business?" she politely asked Shane.

"Business is great! Expansion is happening faster than we anticipated, but I love a challenge," he admitted as he wiped his mouth with his linen napkin. "I don't think Amelia would mind me sharing with everyone that we have decided to throw our hats into the arena at World Tea Expo this June," he announced as he looked around the table.

"Congratulations! I'm so happy for you," Sarah shouted. "What category are you competing in this year?"

"Am I missing something?" Lincoln mused. "Am I the only one who doesn't know about this tea thing?"

"It's called World Tea Expo," I smiled as I patiently explained. "It's held annually in Las Vegas and it showcases the 'best of the best' in the tea world. Renowned speaker come and teach classes like John Harney, Jane Pettigrew and James Norwood Pratt. It's a whole weekend of tea education, tea vendors, and tea competition. It's truly the biggest show for the tea industry," I concluded.

"It's wonderful," Sarah joined in. "People come from all over the world to attend classes, sample beautiful teas and meet some of the people who were fundamental in brining attention to the specialty tea market. I love to go and order supplies for the Pink Dogwood Tea Room. I remember the first time Amelia took me there. We had a wonderful time," she remembered as she took another sip of champagne.

"We did have a good time, didn't we!" I agreed.

"So you're going to have a booth this year?" Cassandra inquired as she took her seat at the head of the table. She scooted in her chair and placed her napkin back in her lap.

"We are going to have exhibit space this year for Smoky Mountain Coffee, Herb and Tea Company as well as compete for the world tea championships," Shane stated proudly.

"They have tea awards? Unbelievable!" Lincoln chuckled. Olivia elbowed him in the ribs playfully trying to get him to be serious.

"Believe it or not, Lincoln, it can be quite cut-throat," Shane informed him.

"I can just see these little old tea ladies heating up their tea kettles shooting evil looks at each other," Lincoln continued to joke.

"Most of the top ranked tea companies are run by men," Sarah said knowledgeably. "There are only a handful of companies with women at the helm."

"I'm going to have to see this for myself to understand," Lincoln continued ribbing Shane.

"Why don't you?" Shane challenged his good friend.

"Why don't I what?" Lincoln asked straight faced.

"Why don't you see if for yourself? Come to Las Vegas in June my friend," Shane offered.

"And stick out my pinky and sip from a tea cup. No offense, old boy, but that's not my cup of tea," he shrugged his shoulders.

"Oh, come on, Lincoln! There's more to do in Vegas besides the Expo. It would be fun!" Olivia beseeched her husband.

"I've seen *The Hangover*. I'm not having one of those Vegas experiences," Lincoln said in all sincerity.

"We stayed at The Venetian Hotel. It was breathtaking! There's so much to see! There are great shows, wonderful restaurants, shopping, sightseeing … you would love it!" Sarah promised.

"I'll think about it," Matt said sipping his champagne and ruffling Olivia's ringlets.

"We could go back out to the Grand Canyon again. Please Matt?" Olivia begged and batted her eyelashes playfully at him.

"It's started," Shane warned his good friend. "Watch her Lincoln. It's hard to say no to your wife," he warned.

"Just what are you trying to say, Shane Spencer?" I intoned.

"Nothing dear, nothing at all!" he responded innocently.

"I think Vegas sounds like a wonderful idea," Cassandra agreed. "I could fly all of us out there. My good friend owns the Wynn Hotel. I'm sure we could reserve some lovely rooms," she recommended.

"Say yes, Lincoln. Please!" Olivia joined in with the others. "It would be like a second honeymoon for us!"

"At World Tea Expo," he reminded her.

"You two could go off and do your own thing," Shane said encouragingly. "We wouldn't want to impede you newlyweds from enjoying yourselves."

"Let's do it! Let's all go!" I said joining in the conspiracy. "To The Traveling Tea Ladies and Las Vegas!" I shouted lifting my champagne flute high in the air.

"To The Traveling Tea Ladies and their dudes!" Sarah chuckled and clinked her glass. "Come on Lincoln have a little fun," she admonished him.

"Give it up, Detective. You're outnumbered," Shane reminded him.

"Ok, ok! Viva Las Vegas!" he agreed and toasted with us. "What have you dragged me into Olivia Rivers Lincoln?" he asked as he kissed her. "What have you dragged me into?"

How to Make
the Perfect Pot of Tea

In the same amount of time that you measure level scoops of coffee for the coffee maker and add ounces of water, you can prepare a cup or pot of tea.

Step 1: Select your tea pot.

Porcelain or pottery is the better choice versus silver plated tea pots which can impart a slightly metallic taste. Make sure your tea pot is clean with no soapy residue and prime your tea pot by filling it with hot water, letting it sit for a few minutes and then pouring the water out so that your pot will stay warm longer!

Step 2: WATER, WATER, WATER!

Begin with the cleanest, filtered, de-chlorinated water you can. Good water makes a huge difference. Many of my tea room guests have asked why their tea doesn't taste the same at home. The chlorine in the water is often the culprit of sabotaging a great pot of tea.

Be sure your water comes to a rolling boil and quickly remove it. If you let it boil continuously, you will boil out all the oxygen and be left with a "flat" tasting tea. Please do not microwave your water. It can cause your water to "super boil" and lead to third degree burns. If you are in a situation where you don't have a full kitchen, purchase an electric tea kettle to quickly and easily make your hot water.

And NEVER, NEVER, EVER MAKE TEA IN A COFFEE MAKER! I cannot tell you how I cringe when asked if it's okay. Coffee drinkers don't want to taste tea and tea drinkers don't want to taste coffee. Period! End of story! Golden rule—no coffee makers!

Now that we've cleared that up, let's measure out our tea!

Step 3: Measure Out Your Tea.

It's easy! The formula is one teaspoon of loose tea per 8 ounces of water. For example, if you are using a 4 cup teapot, you would use 4 teaspoons of tea, maybe a little less depending on your personal taste. Measure your tea and place inside a "t-sac" or paper filter made for tea, infuser ball, or tea filter basket. Place the tea inside your pot and now you're ready for steeping.

Step 4: Steeping Times and Temperature.

This is the key!

> **Black teas**—Steep for 3-4minutes with boiling water (212 degrees)
>
> **Herbals, Tisanes and Rooibos**—boiling water, Steep for 7 minutes.
>
> **Oolongs**—195 degree Water. Steep for 3 minutes.
> **Whites and Greens**—Steaming water—175 degrees. Steep for 3 minutes.

Over steeping any tea will make your tea bitter! Use a timer and get it right. Using water that is too hot for whites and greens will also make your tea bitter!

Got Milk?

Many tea drinkers are under the misconception that cream should be added to your tea, not milk. Actually cream and half-n-half are too heavy. Milk can be added to most black teas and to some oolongs. I don't recommend it for herbals, greens and whites.

The debate continues as to whether to pour milk into your cup before your tea or to add milk after you pour your tea. Really, the decision is yours! I always recommend tasting your tea first before adding milk or any sugar. You would be surprised how perfectly wonderful many teas are without any additions.

I think you're ready to start your tea adventure!

Until Our Next Pot of Tea,

Melanie

Recipes From
The Traveling Tea Ladies
–Till Death Do Us Part

Sarah's Sweetheart Cucumber Sandwiches

"Your tea trays look amazing. What's on the menu today?"

"The heart shaped savories are sweetheart sandwiches. They are filled with a wonderful herb cream cheese spread topped with thinly sliced cucumbers," Sarah said with delight in her voice. —Chapter One.

Sliced white bread-any brand
One eight ounce package of cream cheese
One English cucumber
One bunch green onion
One bunch parsley
One lemon

To prepare herb cream cheese filling:

Bring cream cheese to room temperature (can leave out on counter overnight)

Thinly slice cucumber. I prefer to use a mandolin to make paper thin slices. Cut each slice into fourths to make triangles. Set aside.

Place cream cheese in food processor and pulse for several minutes until cream cheese is smooth.

After thoroughly washing green onion and parsley, finely chop them and add to food processor. Continue pulsing until all ingredients are thoroughly combined.

Add two tablespoons fresh lemon juice to herb and cream cheese mixture. Continue pulsing until thoroughly combined.

*Place bread still in protective packaging in freezer until completely frozen. (Overnight)

Using a heart shaped cookie cutter, cut out center of bread.

Spread thick layer of herb cream cheese on heart cut out.

Overlap three cucumber triangles in center of heart, pointed side towards bottom of bread. Serve immediately!

*Freezing bread makes cut outs very easy. You can do multiple cutouts in advance and re-freeze in plastic baggies until your next tea party. I have experimented with whole grain and whole wheat bread, but I prefer white bread for the cucumber sandwiches

Note from Melanie: These little sandwiches are highly addictive, so watch out! I often found myself long after the tea room guests had left sitting on the back porch with a very thick layer of herb cream cheese topped with thousands of cucumbers sandwiched between bread enjoying "my moment." This spread is wonderful on crackers topped with fresh sliced cherry tomatoes. I allow the herb cream cheese to come to room temperature to make spreading the filling easier.

Red and Yellow Pepper Mini Quiches

"They are gorgeous! You are so creative," I said in awe. "And the individual yellow and red pepper quiches complement the table color scheme perfectly." —Chapter One

6 eggs

2 cups milk or half-n-half

2-3 cups of your favorite cheese

1 sweet red pepper, finely chopped

1 yellow pepper, finely chopped

Dash of nutmeg

Salt & pepper to taste

VIP brand mini tart shells (freezer section in dessert aisle)

Preheat oven to 350 degrees for 25 minutes or more.

In a large mixing bowl, whisk eggs.

Add milk and continue whisking.

Add cheese, nutmeg, salt and pepper.

Place tart shells on baking sheet. Fill with egg mixture and bake for 25 minutes or until firm in center. Remove from aluminum tart pan and serve hot.

Note from Melanie: I have tried several brands of pre-made mini pie shells and these are my personal favorite. They have a braided edge which really makes them stand out on the tea tray. Can be frozen and stored in airtight containers.

Smoked Turkey and Cranberry Mini Panini

"I'm also serving mini smoked turkey and cranberry Panini's with a tea cup filled with butternut squash soup."
—Chapter One

Sliced sourdough bread-bakery quality
Whole cranberry sauce, such as Ocean Spray
Deli quality smoked turkey, thinly sliced
Herb Cream Cheese Spread (See Sarah's Sweetheart Cucumber Sandwiches)
Red onion, thinly sliced

Spread herb cream cheese on one slice of sourdough bread.

Layer 3-4 slices of turkey on top of herb cream cheese.

Spread one tablespoon of cranberry sauce on another slice of sourdough bread.

Top with thinly sliced red onion.

Place bread slices together.

Using a sandwich maker or Panini grill, sear sandwich until bread is toasted and warm.

Cut in half and then cut each half into long rectangular thirds.

Note from Melanie: These sandwiches were on our lunch menu at Miss Melanie's Tea Room. The flavor combination of cranberry, red onion and herb cream cheese cannot be beat. It makes a delicious and colorful sandwich!

Cranberry Orange Scones

"I love the flavor combination. They are beautiful!" I told Sarah as she pulled them out of the double ovens. The scones had puffed up and split in the middle. "I think this bridal tea is going to be just the thing to ease Olivia's tensions."
—Chapter One

2 cups all-purpose flour

2 teaspoons baking powder

½ teaspoon salt

¼ cup granulated sugar

1 stick unsalted butter

½ cup dried cranberry

2 eggs

2 tablespoons orange juice

Zest of one orange

1 tablespoon vanilla extract

2 tablespoons cane sugar for topping

Preheat oven to 400 degree. Place parchment paper or silicone baking pad on baking sheet pan.

In a large mixing bowl combine flour, baking powder, sugar, and salt.

Cut in butter with a pastry blender until mixture resembles coarse crumbs.

Add dried cranberries and orange zest.

In a small bowl, whisk together eggs, orange juice and vanilla.

Add wet mixture to flour mixture, stirring quickly to combine. The dough will be very sticky.

Turn dough out on a lightly floured surface. Using a rolling pin, roll out to 1-1.5 inch thickness.

Using a floured round biscuit cutter, gently insert straight into dough and lift straight up being careful not to twist (that will cause a break in air bubbles and the result will be a flat looking scone.)

Place scones on baking sheet. Sprinkle cane sugar on top. Bake for 23-25 minutes. Scones will rise high and should split.

Note from Melanie: I like to freeze my unbaked scones right on the baking sheet for at least 2-3 hours. The freezing process helps to ensure a "higher" baking scone. You can freeze them and store in freezer bags until ready to use so you can have a tea party anytime when unexpected company drops by!

Olivia's Organic Orange Honey Butter

"I haven't even shown you my scones yet! Wait until you sink your teeth into these beauties-cranberry orange with orange honey butter. Pure bliss!" she bragged. "The organic white clover honey is from Olivia's bee hives at Riverbend Ranch." —Chapter One.

1 stick unsalted organic butter

Zest of one organic orange

¼ cup organic honey

Soften butter to room temperature.

In a mixing bowl, combine all ingredients. Using the paddle attachment, whip until butter is smooth and all ingredients are thoroughly combined.

This butter is best served at room temperature with scones hot out of the oven. It can be stored in the refrigerator for up to two weeks.

Note from Melanie: This recipe is dedicated to Sonya Crago who claims she is the "real Olivia" (She is a red head by the way). She and her husband have an organic farm outside Chattanooga and provide organic honey, eggs and beef for sale. For more information about ordering Sonya's organic white clover honey, please refer to my resource guide at the back of the book.

Amelia's Meyer Lemon and Chamomile Tea Meringue Pies

"I've brought my Meyer lemon and chamomile tea meringue pies and our latest iced tea blend." —Chapter Five

Lemon-Chamomile Cream Filling:

3 cups whole milk

3-4 tablespoons loose chamomile tea

¼ cup cornstarch

1 cup sugar

¼ teaspoon salt

4 large egg yolks

1½ teaspoons lemon zest

¼ cup fresh-squeezed lemon juice

4 tablespoons unsalted butter, softened

Meringue:

4 large egg whites

1 cup plus 2 tablespoons sugar

½ teaspoon vanilla extract

¼ teaspoon cream of tartar

Pinch of salt

To make the Cream Filling:

Bring milk to a boil in a medium saucepan. Remove from heat. Place loose tea in paper tea filter and add directly to the hot milk. Cover saucepan with lid. Steep for 5 minutes. Discard tea filter.

Combine cornstarch, sugar, and ¼ teaspoon salt in a medium saucepan. Add the tea-infused milk and whisk. Turn up heat to medium-high and stir constantly , until mixture is bubbling thick and coats the spatula. (About seven minutes).

Whisk yolks in a separate bowl, then pour in the milk mixture into the yolks very slowly, whisking until incorporated (using a tempering method). Return the mixture to the saucepan and continue cooking over medium heat, stirring constantly, until it returns to a boil. Continue cooking for an additional 1 to 2 minutes.

Remove the custard mixture from heat. Stir in lemon zest and juice. Add butter, 1 tablespoon at a time, stirring until butter melts. Then add the next piece. Let cool in the saucepan away from heat, whisking occasionally, for up to 10 minutes.

Pour custard into the prepared crust. Press plastic wrap directly on surface of custard, taking care to smooth out any wrinkles.

Refrigerate at least 4 hours (or overnight) so that the custard filling is chilled and firm.

To make the Meringue:

Make the meringue topping just before serving. Combine egg whites and sugar in a glass or stainless mixing bowl set over a saucepan of simmering water. Whisk until the sugar dissolves and the mixture is warm (about 3 minutes). Remove from heat and add vanilla, cream of tartar, and a pinch of salt. Whisk the mixture on medium-high speed until shiny, stiff peaks form, about 7 minutes. Carefully bake the meringue-topped pie briefly on a baking sheet under a broiler until lightly golden. Serve immediately.

Cassandra's Mo Jo Mojitos

"Cassandra is bringing the Mojitos. It's going to be a fun afternoon and evening!" —Chapter Five.

1 1/2 parts ABSOLUT Vodka Wild Tea
3/4 part Fresh Lime Juice
1/2 part Simple Syrup
4 Mint Leaves
SodaWater

Muddle mint leaves with simple syrup and lime juice in a shaker. Add ABSOLUT Wild Tea. Shake and pour into a highball glass. Top with soda.

Aunt Imogene's Southern Caviar-Deviled Eggs

Aunt Imogene had brought her party staple-deviled eggs which are like southern caviar to our family and Lucy had brought a hummingbird cake. —Chapter Seven.

6 large eggs

2 tablespoons mayonnaise (I like Duke's or Hellman's)

1 ½ teaspoon sweet pickle relish

1 teaspoon Dijon mustard

1 teaspoon salt

Dash of white pepper

Garnish: Spanish paprika and chives

Place eggs in a single layer in saucepan.

Add water to depth of 3 inches.

Bring to a boil. Cover saucepan, remove from heat and let stand for 15 minutes.

Drain immediately and fill saucepan with cold water and ice.

Tap each egg on the counter until cracks form all over shell.

Peel eggs under cold running water

Slice eggs lengthwise with serrated knife.

Carefully remove yolks. Mash yolks and combine with mayonnaise, pickle relish, mustard, salt and pepper. Stir and mash until smooth.

Fill a sandwich baggie with yolk mixture. Snip small hole in corner and pipe yolk into egg whites or if you prefer, use a pastry bag with a decorative tip.

Garnish with paprika and snipped chives.

Note from Melanie: I always serve these on my Grandmother's antique deviled egg tray. Whenever the tray is full, I enjoy eating the extras! They don't last long at our house. I would not fill the egg whites until just before serving. I'm sure you have your own version of our "southern caviar." Some folks like to add chopped onion and bacon. Perfect for any tea tray, picnic, or BBQ.

Miss Melanie's Tea Room Famous Greek Pasta Salad

The tri-colored pasta was combined with Kalamata olives, sweet red onions, green peppers, chunks of feta cheese, and cherry tomatoes with a homemade Greek dressing.
—Chapter Nineteen.

One box tri colored pasta spirals

8 ounces crumbled feta

Small red onion, finely chopped

Small green pepper, finely chopped

Pint of cherry tomatoes cut in halves

Small jar of Kalamata olives, finely chopped

Italian seasoning to taste

One bottle of your favorite Greek salad dressing

Cook pasta according to directions and rinse with cold water for several minutes. Allow to completely cool.

Add all ingredients and toss gently. Refrigerate until ready to serve.

Note from Melanie: One of my all-time favorite recipes. This recipe can be made into a main dish meal with the addition of grilled chicken or albacore tuna. Love it, love it, love it!

Legendary Lemonade Party Cake

"Don't forget to grab a slice of lemonade cake," she reminded everyone as they moved through the line.

"My favorite!" Shane grinned as he helped himself to a slice. The tart cake was layered with a sweet lemon glaze made from concentrated lemonade and confectioner's sugar. A coconut whipped cream frosting topped the yummy dessert. —Chapter Nineteen.

1 box moist lemon cake mix

3 eggs

1 cup water

½ cup Olive oil

Frozen Lemonade Concentrate

½ cup Confectioners' Sugar (Powdered Sugar)

1 Pint Heavy whipping cream

3 Tablespoons Vanilla extract or Almond Extract

(I prefer almond with lemon)

1-2 cups Shredded Coconut

Heat Oven to 350 degrees

Prepare cake mix according to directions on box combining mix, eggs, water and oil. Beat at medium speed with a mixer for two minutes until all ingredients are combined.

Pour batter into greased 9X11 baking pan or two round 8 inch cake pans. Bake for 35 minutes or until toothpick inserted in center comes out clean.

While cake is baking, combine half of frozen lemonade concentrate with confectioner's sugar forming yummy syrup. Whisk together until incorporated. Taste test to make sure the balance of sweet and tart is to your liking. Often times, I find I add more sugar to get it just right.

When cake is pulled out of oven, immediately poke holes all surface using a toothpick. Pour lemonade/sugar syrup over top of cake making sure syrup flows into the holes. Allow to completely cool.

While cake is cooling, in a large bowl combine pint of whipping cream with vanilla or almond extract and confectioner's sugar. Using an electric mixer, whip all ingredients together until cream begins to thicken. Increase mixer speed to high and whip until soft peaks form.

Spread whipped cream mixture on top of cooled cake. Sprinkle liberally with coconut. Refrigerate until ready to serve.

Note from Melanie: You can't beat the combination of lemon, almond and coconut for a refreshing dessert. It's light, tangy and delicious. If you would like to increase the lemon flavor, turn this recipe into a layer cake using homemade lemon curd for filling.

Apple Thyme Cocktail

"Servers presented guests with fall cocktails designed for the affair. They were made with a thyme infused simple syrup, apple cider and apple brandy garnished with a fresh slice of apple." —Chapter Twenty-Three

This wonderful recipe is adapted from the Gramercy Tavern in New York City.

Thyme simple syrup:

  1/4 cup sugar

  1/4 cup water

  4 sprigs fresh thyme

Cocktail:

  1 ounce bourbon

  1 ounce calvados or apple brandy

  1 ounce fresh apple cider

  1/2 ounce thyme simple syrup

  1/2 ounce freshly squeezed lemon juice

  Dash of bitters

  Garnish: dried or fresh apple slice

Place sugar and water in small saucepan over medium heat stirring continually until sugar completely dissolves.

Remove from heat and add sprigs of fresh thyme.

Place lid on saucepan and steep for 15 minutes or longer, tasting for intensity of flavor. Strain out thyme. Refrigerate to chill

Fill a cocktail shaker with ice.

Add bourbon, calvados or apple brandy, cider, thyme syrup, lemon, and bitters.

Shake and strain into a chilled martini glass.

Garnish with fresh or dried apple if desired.

Note from Melanie: This cocktail has a warm golden color and makes a beautiful addition to a fall party. Cheers!

Resource Guide

I admit it, I am shamelessly addicted to weddings; wedding dresses, wedding shows, wedding magazines, wedding flowers! It's an obsession I share with my daughter Olivia, so naturally she was thrilled to have her character get married in The Traveling Tea Ladies Till Death Do Us Part. We poured over websites and watched a few weddings on television to get us in the proper mood to create the backdrop for this fun read.

Over the years, we hosted many bridal teas at Miss Melanie's Tea Room and I enjoyed watching the excitement in the bride's eyes as she opened her gifts or shared her last get together with friends before the big event. It was always a happy occasion to plan a special afternoon tea in the bride's honor.

I hope I have given you some ideas of how to plan a tea party for your next bridal event or how to plan a downhome ranch wedding. Tennessee, in my humble opinion, has some of the most breathtaking vistas anywhere. I've included some websites of great venues and vendors to recreate a wedding just like Olivia and Lincoln's.

Until Our Next Pot of Tea,

Melanie

Brumleys Restaurant

111 North Main Street, Greeneville, Tennessee 37743

Located inside the historic General Morgan Inn, each room has a unique ambiance. A truly wonderful dining experience.

(423) 787-7500

Carrington Acres Farm

340 Old Freewill Drive, Cleveland, Tennessee 37311

Specializing in premium beef, honey and eggs, Sonya and Brent Crago offer products that are "all natural," free of hormones, steroids, antibiotics and animal by-products.

www.CaringtonAcres.com (423) 339-0094

Abram's Falls

Near Townsend, Tennessee, one of the most beautiful hiking destinations in the Great Smoky Mountains National Park.

www.HikingintheSmokys.com/Abrams.htm

Small Miracle's Therapeutic Horse Back Riding Center

1026 Rock Springs Drive, Kingsport, Tennessee

www.small-miracles.org (423) 349-1111

Austin Springs Spa

1216 West State of Franklin Road, Johnson City, Tennessee 37659

A favorite spot for pampering for the bride and the entire wedding party located in the Carnegie Hotel.

www.AustinSpringsSpa.com (423-979-6403)

St. John's Mill
3191 Watauga Road, Watauga, Tennessee 37694

Tennessee's oldest business founded in 1770 has a colorful history. In 1784, the area was claimed by North Carolina, and later considered part of the State of Franklin. Finally in 1796, it was brought into Tennessee when the state was ratified. All 232 years, the business has remained in the same bloodline. It is now part of the historic St. John's Foundation.

East Tennessee State Blue Grass Band
Keeping our Appalachian heritage honored, East Tennessee State University offers the only program with degrees available in storytelling, bluegrass and Irish studies. Please visit YouTube for videos of this wonderful addition to our mountain community.

http://www.etsu.edu/das/bluegrass

World Tea Expo
Dedicated to creating a vibrant community, World Tea Expo is the largest trade show and conference in the world for premium tea and related products; it's the three days each year when industry professionals connect face-to-face to unveil new products, optimize high quality merchandise, gain in-depth product knowledge and network with peers.

www.WorldTeaExpo.com

Smoky Mountain Coffee, Herb & Tea Company

Official Tea Company of The Traveling Tea Ladies Murder Mystery Books featuring organic coffees and teas, gifts and autographed books. Interested in purchasing one of the teas featured in this book? A complete collection of teas from all The Traveling Tea Ladies are available for purchase as well as a line of tea gift baskets and apparel.

www.SmokyMountainCoffee-Herb-Tea.com

The Tea Academy

Consulting and Training for Tea Professionals. Join Melanie for "Tea Tours" of your favorite tea destinations or organize a group and plan a customized tour.

www.TheTeaAcademy.com (423) 926-0123

Wedding Venues & Vendors

Event Barn Center of the Smokies

7264 East Lamar Alexander Parkway, Townsend, Tennessee
The cantilever barn and award winning gardens make this a picture perfect backdrop for your wedding.

www.BarnEventCenteroftheSmokies.com
(865) 448-3812

Pleasant Hill Vineyards

2728 Wilkinson Pike, Maryville, Tennessee 37803
Surrounded by mountain views, vineyards and rolling countryside, Pleasant Hill Vineyards is the perfect wedding venue located close to Maryville and Knoxville, Tennessee.

www.PleasantHillVineyards.com (865) 984-1530

Harvest Acres Farm

357 Harvest Lane, Limestone, Tennessee 37681

Planning an outdoor wedding or reception in a beautiful barn? From bonfires to hayrides, Harvest Acres Farm can accommodate up to two hundred guests in style.

www.HarvestAcresFarm.com (423) 361-5289

The Lily Barn

1116 Carrs Creek Road, Townsend, Tennessee 37882

Specializing in garden weddings, exchange your "I Dos" surrounded by thousands of daylilies. From the cake, to the flowers, to the entertainment pavilion, The Lily Barn will make your dream wedding a unique event.

www.LilyBarn.com (865) 448-9895

The General Morgan Inn

111 North Main Street, Greeneville, Tennessee 37743

This is the perfect location for a sophisticated wedding reception with historic charm located in downtown Greeneville, Tennessee.

www.GeneralMorganInn.com (423) 787-1000

Carnegie Hotel

1216 West State of Franklin Road, Johnson City, Tennessee, 37659

This landmark hotel provides a beautiful backdrop for your stylish wedding reception. From the wedding cake to the elegant seated dinner, this hotel aims to please with high marks for service and ambiance.

www.CarnegieHotel.com 1-888-743-0509

David Clapp Photography

David offers his gift of interpretive and sensitive imaging to clients from all over the country.

www.DavidClapp.com (423) 378-5044

Magpie's Wedding Cakes

Beautiful customized wedding cakes for your dream day or special occasion.

www.MagPiesCakes.com (865) 673-0471

Whimsical Gatherings

From soirees, to weddings, to holiday parties, this designer team will make your vision come to life.

www.WhimisicalGatherings.com (865) 256-0701

Swallow Tail Farms

Beautiful butterfly release packages as well as unique wedding favors and invitations.

www.SwallowTailFarms.com

Profile in Time

Create your personalized wedding logo using your silhouette! Featuring stationary, gift tags, invitations, cupcakes, cookies and more.

www.ProfileinTime.com

About the Author

Former tea room owner, Melanie O'Hara, is a graduate of Southern Methodist University and East Tennessee State University. Her love of tea was ignited after a semester abroad studying international communications in London, England.

She shares her passion with people inspired to follow their tea dreams through her Tea Academy classes and tea tours.

Melanie, her husband Keith and their brood of children make their home in East Tennessee. When she is not writing, conducting a tea lecture, giving a cooking with tea demonstration or leading a tea tour, you can find her at the helm of her online business, Smoky Mountain Coffee, Herb & Tea Company.

For more information about The Tea Academy, booking your own tea tour, or attending a tea class, e-mail Melanie.

Melanie@TheTravelingTeaLadies.com

And join her tea adventure on Facebook where the tea party never ends!

LYONS
LEGACY
PUBLISHING™

Traveling Tea Ladies readers, for other Lyons Legacy titles you may enjoy, or to purchase other books in The Traveling Tea Ladies Series, signed by the author, visit our website:

www.LyonsLegacyPublishing.com